D1622900

D__ ll
Brothers

DATE DUE

BRODART, CO.   Cat. No. 23-221-003

W M / KIDS / 4   White Mane Publishing Company, Inc.

ED
B622B

This White Mane Publishing Company, Inc. publication was printed by Beidel Printing House, Inc.
63 West Burd Street
Shippensburg, PA 17257 USA

In respect for the scholarship contained herein, the acid-free paper used in this book meets the guidelines for permanence and durability of the Committee on Production Guidelines for Book Longevity of the Council on Library Resources.

For a complete list of available publications please write:
White Mane Publishing Company, Inc.
P. O. Box 152
Shippensburg, PA 17257-0152

Library of Congress Cataloging-in-Publication Data

Blair, Margaret Whitman.
    Brothers at war / Margaret Whitman Blair.
        p.   cm.
    Summary: Rob and Jamie, brothers who are opposites and who are both involved in a Civil War reenactment, find themselves transported back in time to the actual Antietam campaign in 1862.
    ISBN 1-57249-049-7 (alk. paper)
    1. Antietam, Battle of, Md., 1862--Juvenile fiction.
[1. Antietam, Battle of, Md., 1862--Fiction. 2. United States--History--Civil War, 1862–1865--Fiction. 3. Time travel--Fiction.]
I. Title.
PZ7.B537864Br   1997
[Fic]--dc21   96-45384
                                                               CIP
                                                                AC

PRINTED IN THE UNITED STATES OF AMERICA

Dedication

For my beloved David and Matthew—brothers who are usually best friends and only occasionally at war.

Table of Contents

Acknowledgements

I want to especially thank my son Matthew, whose youthful enthusiasm for the Civil War inspired me to plunge once again into that historic conflict—and who read each chapter directly after it was written with his sharp and ever vigilant eyes. Many thanks also to my other young readers—most especially to Alicia, Jeff, Jessie, Joseph, and Navy—who gave me frank advice as well as enthusiasm.

I could not have written this without the assistance of many Civil War reenactors, in particular the generous contributions of Robert Lee Hodge, Brian Pohanka, Mike Thompson, Susan Vavrick and Cricket Bauer. Special thanks to my many writer friends who gave me invaluable input and moral support, especially Steve Taylor, Dennis Wrynn, Jack Kaufman, Jean Lawrence, Robert Calambokidis, Miriam Ruff, Rick Umbaugh, and Janet Brown.

And of course a most loving thanks to Bob, my better half, my severest critic yet my biggest fan, who supports me in all ways forever.

Chapter 1

Artillery Hell

Rob tensed every muscle, waiting for the mighty boom of the cannon. It was the anticipation of it, not the actual sound itself, that was the worst. BOOM. A sheet of flame belched from the cannon. Smoke swirled in front of him, further clouding his vision in the already murky half-light of dawn.

Again, the cannon roared. This time, the cannon's force threw him to the ground. He lay there for a moment, flexing muscle groups, checking to see if he was all right. Yes, he was all right—no injuries.

Back and forth, back and forth, the cannons played a deadly duel. "Artillery hell," Rob thought. The sound was deafening. Soon the entire field was wreathed in giant rings of smoke.

"Load and come to the ready, men." Hearing the command, Rob forced his body to move. This was no time for fear! Rolling over onto his belly, he bit open a fresh cartridge and rammed its contents down the muzzle of his weapon, all the while watching the men in blue advance through the cornfield toward him. "Fightin' Joe" Hooker's men, moving in double lines, like blue ghosts in the gray dawn.

His captain's voice rang out. "Aim . . . fire!" Rob fired together with the other men in gray. He watched the blue figures fall. Not bad for a sixteen-year-old rookie. He reloaded, faster this time. If he squinted through the smoke-shrouded sunlight, he could just barely make out a drummer boy, way over on the Yanks' right flank, beating time for the advancing troops. Rob shifted his weapon until his brother's form was squarely in his line of vision.

"Fire!"

Down went the drummer boy, the rattling of his drums stilled. Crumpled like a rag doll, lying limply on the ground. Rob smiled in grim satisfaction.

The voice of his captain intruded.

"Not bad for a dry run. But let's try to fire at the same time, shall we? And you with the big slouch hat, you're new to our unit, aren't you? What's your name again, private?"

"Rob Henry . . . sir!"

"Why were you aiming at the right flank, Henry? I wanted you men firing on the center, not the flanks. All right, break for lunch. Bloody Lane begins at 2 p.m. sharp. For those of you who aren't in camp, there's a McDonald's down Route 11."

His cheeks burning with embarrassment, Rob walked over to Jamie's side of the field. Jamie was still lying there in the wet morning grass like a crumpled-up soldier doll. Rob hadn't realized his choice of target had been so obvious. He stood above the target now, looking down at Jamie's light blue eyes staring up at an equally blue sky. He had to admit, blue was his color. And the kid wasn't bad at playing dead. Only one thing ruined the image: he was wearing head-phones! Listening to rap music . . . at a Civil War battle reenactment. How disgustingly inappropriate! Rob kicked Jamie's drum. No response. Rob gave a soft jab with his musket.

"Ouch!"

Jamie looked up, annoyed.

Rob gave him another jab, a little harder. This time he got him to remove the headphones.

"Get up, Yankee scum! That was the worst dying I've ever seen. And put away that Walkman. You're really embarrassing me with your anachronisms. You know they didn't have Sony Walkmans in the nineteenth century!"

Jamie rolled lazily onto his side. As usual, it looked like he was ready for a nap. Jamie yawned, slowly tucking the headphones into his haversack.

"You're just jealous 'cause you know I can do a better bloat than you." He exhaled until his stomach stuck way out, then puffed up his cheeks in demonstration of a two-day old corpse. "Speaking of bloat, let's hitch a ride over to Mac's. Your treat."

Rob looked at his brother's lanky body in disgust. Although two years younger, Jamie already towered over his "big" brother. If Jamie ever stopped growing like a weed, he would surely turn into a butterball—all that junk food and the way he avoided any unnecessary movement. Rob, on the other hand, was careful about what he ate, lifted weights and jogged daily, and yet he still was one of the smallest guys in his class. And, most annoying, whenever they met somebody new, it was always assumed that Jamie was the older brother.

"If you just want junk food, you can find it here. I can smell greasy hamburgers cooking over at the sutler's camp."

Jamie laughed and got to his feet.

"Beef jerky and hardtack for you, Mr. 'Hard-core.'"

****

The Henry Brothers—the tall red-haired boy dressed in blue, his shorter, dark-haired sibling in gray—walked side by side. They walked past the soldier reenactors' tents toward those of the merchant sutlers. Men in uniforms sauntered past them, weapons slung over their shoulders. An occasional cavalry officer, looking dashing in a fine feathered hat, galloped by as if on urgent business. The notes of "Dixie," played on a harmonica, floated through the air.

The sight of all the white canvas tents, row upon row of them all the way down the hill, excited Rob's imagination. He could imagine it really was an army camp and the merchants were sutlers from the 1860's, plying their overpriced wares to Civil War soldiers. If only people wouldn't park their cars so close to the camp—now that really spoiled the mood!

A group of laughing teenaged girls, dressed in hoop skirts and bonnets, baskets on their arms, caught the boys' attention. Jamie almost walked into a tree he was so busy watching them.

"Looking for somebody?" asked Rob, his voice sharper than he had intended.

"Not really."

"'Cause if you are, she told me she probably wouldn't be coming."

Jamie shrugged his shoulders. "Maybe that's not what she told me . . . Hey, Billy!" He waved at a Union reenactor walking past them. "Your gear looks totally awesome!"

The man beamed. "Thanks, Jamie."

Jamie had been a "walk-on"—he had not even registered as part of a regular unit—and yet already he seemed to know half the men at the reenactment. "I wish you'd stop using slang. It sounds so modern," complained Rob.

Jamie laughed at him. "Oh, go back to the nineteenth century." But before Rob could retort, Jamie was waving at another group. Here came a bunch of "Zouave" soldiers, one of the New York units, dressed in baggy scarlet trousers, with red fezzes perched on their heads.

"Brian, Joe, Sam . . . lookin' good, guys!" They waved their hats at him, pleased at the compliment.

"Ridiculous uniform!" snorted Rob. "No wonder they got creamed at Second Manassas! Talk about a good target!"

Jamie's roving eyes stopped searching. Rob followed his gaze to a group of hoop-skirted beauties standing at a food stand. The sunlight bounced off familiar golden-red hair. Rob's heart jumped into his throat so hard he could barely swallow.

But Jamie was never at a loss for words. He gave a loud drum roll and his whistle was so loud it could be heard for miles. And then that wisecracking, slightly hoarse voice of his carried across the crowd. "Sarah Singleton! You look bee-yoo-ti-ful today!"

****

Chapter 2

Sarah Singleton

Even before Jamie spoke, Sarah turned her head, as if she knew the drum roll and whistle were for her. For though many girls at school had pretty faces and cute figures, Sarah even at fourteen had a kind of brilliance that made her stand out. Whistles were often aimed in her direction.

Rob stood still as a statue of Stonewall Jackson. Sarah Singleton, not in blue jeans but dressed as a Southern belle—this was the girl of his dreams! Her green eyes matched the shining plaid hoop skirt which swirled around her as she turned, her long hair pulled into a bun and covered with a golden net, her pale throat encircled by a white collar on which a brilliant broach glinted in the sunlight.

Rob's head grew dizzy with images. Rob and Sarah walking hand in hand up an old plantation drive. Sarah fluttering a lacy handkerchief in farewell as Rob rode off to war on his big white horse. Tears slowly trickling down Sarah's pale cheeks as she read in a telegram that Rob Henry had been killed at Sharpsburg.

Meanwhile, Jamie moved uncharacteristically fast. He pushed his way to the front of the line at the food stand where Sarah stood and threw several dollar bills on the counter. "A pretty lady should never have to spend her own money," he said.

Sarah slipped the money back to Jamie. "I pay my own way, James Henry. I don't like to owe anyone." But she softened her words by throwing him one of her dazzling smiles, like a gift she gave only to special people.

Rob felt a stab of jealousy, as he watched Sarah sip her lemonade and continue to smile up at Jamie. While he had been daydreaming, Jamie had taken action. Those smiles should have been directed at him, not his slow-moving brother! He turned his head away. He could feel the hot tears welling up in his eyes and he didn't want Jamie to see that.

The scent of sunflowers drifted near and he felt a satiny sleeve brush against his arm. His heart beat faster as Sarah linked her arm in his, but then, he noticed, she placed her other arm in Jamie's, as they strolled down the gravel path.

"Let's do some shopping. You need a new hat, Rob. That old slouch hat of yours is absolutely filthy."

Rob flushed, but while he tried to think up a snappy response, Jamie had beaten him to it again.

"Oh, don't touch that! He deliberately rolls it in the mud to give it that authentic battle-scarred look."

Sarah laughed with that infectious, musical laugh of hers, making Rob blush even more.

"Besides, he can't go shopping! He's got to go back to camp to fry his hardtack in bacon fat for lunch."

"Yum, yum!" She laughed again. But she gave Rob's arm a little squeeze.

She steered them toward a tent with an old-fashioned handwritten sign posted over the entrance: "The Mule Shoe."

"Let's go in here," she said. "Maybe I can find new shoes while you're looking at hats."

She may be a straight A student, but she's got a lot to learn about the Civil War, Rob thought. He cleared his throat to launch his lecture.

"Has nothing to do with shoes. May 12, 1864." His voice had turned deep and scholarly like a historian's. "Fifth day of the Battle of Spotsylvania. The Rebs entrenched in a 'V' formation. The northernmost point of that 'V' they called the Mule Shoe. Union troops threw themselves at the Rebs with everything they had. Rebs held fast. Hand-to-hand fighting in pouring rain for almost twenty hours—fighting so fierce they called it the 'Bloody Angle.'"

He stole a glance at Sarah to see if he had bored her with his lecture.

"You know so much about the Civil War," she said, batting her long golden eyelashes at him.

She moved to a table stacked with Union and Confederate caps, then playfully pulled off Rob's slouch hat and planted a clean new kepi of gray wool on him instead.

"Sarah, don't!" He threw the new cap back on the table and snatched his old hat back. "I always wear this!" He put it on his head, pulling its rim down at the correct angle. "This is an original. My great-great-great-grandfather wore it at Sharpsburg." He looked at the stack of factory-made caps stacked on the table and his lip curled in disgust. "These new hats are 'farb.'"

He hoped Sarah knew what that meant: "far be it from authentic"—the worst possible insult for a serious Civil War reenactor.

Rebuffed by Rob, she tried one of the hats on Jamie, who pulled the cap low over his forehead.

"Very handsome," she murmured.

That smile again. Rob watched as Jamie watched her perfect lips curve upward in approval.

Rob sensed a moment of intimacy between his brother and his lady love. He must distract them at once! He turned in desperation to find another sutler's tent to interest them, anything to pull their eyes away from each other.

Some ornate silver writing caught his eye. "QUICK-SILVER IMAGES. Relive the Past through the Magic of Authentic Civil War Photographs."

"Come on, you guys! Let's have our picture taken!"

Rob pushed Jamie and Sarah down the gravel path in the direction of the QUICKSILVER IMAGES tent.

"Our pictures taken? What a wonderful idea!" She winked at Rob. "I mean, you boys both look so dashing in your uniforms!"

Two can play that game, Rob thought. "No, Sarah. It's you I want the picture of. You're so beautiful in that dress."

Jamie shot him a dirty look as Rob smiled in triumph. Score one to two. Maybe he could catch up.

"You should smile more often," Sarah said. "You look so handsome when you do."

"Yeah, he's normally such a grouch," Jamie added. "Hey, do we even have time for a picture? Bloody Lane starts at two. You wouldn't want to miss one of the high points of the Battle of Antietam, would you?"

Rob glared at him. "It won't take long. And it's called the Battle of Sharpsburg."

"Only if you're a Rebel. You're suppposed to name battles after the nearest body of water. Antietam Creek."

"Sharpsburg," insisted Rob. "You name the battle after the nearest town."

"Antietam," said Jamie.

"Sharpsburg," Rob muttered between clenched teeth.

"Would you guys please stop fighting?" admonished Sarah. "We're in Maryland. Not Northern or Southern. So it doesn't matter which name, does it now?"

Jamie pulled back the flap of the tent. "Knock, knock! Anybody home?"

The tent appeared to be empty. Jamie turned to go.

"Wait!" Rob stopped them. Pointing to a row of photographs hanging on one of the tent walls, he pulled them inside. They stared at faded amber images of soldiers in uniform proudly holding their muskets and sabers. "These are real Civil War photographs!"

"No way!" argued Jamie. "They're imitations. You shouldn't be so gullible."

"Me, gullible? That's a laugh," retorted Rob, stung. "Hey, look, some of these pictures look just like the original Mathew Brady pictures. Like this one of Bloody Lane!"

SWOOOSH. The sound of a curtain being sharply pulled back startled them. A big bearded man with a large head and long dark hair emerged from a smaller, black curtained tent in the rear of the larger tent. They had been so absorbed in their arguing they had not even noticed it. As the man drew the small black tent's curtains closed behind him, they saw a sign posted, "KEEP OUT! PRIVATE! NO TRESPASSING!"

The man was dressed in a smock coat over black pants and a vest, and the buttons strained over his broad barreled chest. His stern square face broke into a smile at seeing he had customers. At least Rob thought it was a smile, but he wasn't quite sure since the man's mouth was completely covered by his drooping moustache and full beard. His penetrating dark eyes now stared as if he were already composing them into a picture inside his head.

"Well! And what a charming trio of reenactors have come to visit me!" He spoke with a strong Scottish brogue, his r's rough as sandpaper, as he rubbed his large stained hands together. "It is such a pleasure to photograph people who really look the'rr roles." The dark eyes suddenly became anxious. "You do want to be photographed, do you not?"

"Yes, of course." If Sarah liked the idea, Rob was definitely going to push it. "But my brother here and I were having a disagreement."

"Yeah, for a change," muttered Jamie.

Rob ignored him. "Are these original Civil War photographs hanging on the wall here? Or did you take them?"

The man smiled modestly. Or maybe smiled. "Not bad, are they?"

Jamie hit his brother on the arm. "See, I told you they weren't the real thing."

Rob wasn't convinced. "But . . . they look so real. And where did you get that picture of Bloody Lane with all the dead soldiers?"

The man in the smock held up a hand to interrupt him. "Allow me to tell you how I recreate the past." He pointed to an ancient camera mounted on a tripod. "I use an actual camera from the period. First I coat a glass plate with a mixture of collodion." He pointed toward the dark tent. "Then I submerge the coated plate in a bath of iodide of silver. That takes about two minutes. It must be done in absolute darkness . . . ."

Rob started to move toward the black tent. "Oh, you mean this is your darkroom?"

Alarmed, the photographer blocked his path. "Do not go in that tent!" Sarah gave him a funny look. "I mean, you could ruin me pictures, lad. I must have total darkness both for preparin' the negative and for the actual development process."

He motioned them over to a cushioned bench. "Sit yourselves down a minute while I prepare the plates."

Sarah hesitated. "I don't know if we should. We don't even know your name. Or how much your pictures cost."

"Don't worry about the cost, Sarah," Jamie said. "It's on me."

"I told you I like to pay my own way," she said. But she sat down.

The man handed Sarah his card with its fancy silver writing. "QUICKSILVER IMAGES. Authentic Civil War photographs by Alexander G." She turned over the card suspiciously. "No last name? And where's your address and phone number?"

Alexander gave her that half smile and his eyes held a touch of mockery. "Oh, anyone can find me at the battles. I'm easy to find. And here is the price list."

"Holy moly! That's expensive!" Jamie blurted out.

Alexander looked anxious. "Well, perhaps I can charge as if you were one person. That is, if you all were to pose together for the one picture."

Jamie put one arm around Sarah and one around Rob. "Hey, that's cool. We're just one happy family here."

Rob moved away slightly. "Yeah, right." He looked at Sarah. "Okay, Alexander, you have yourself a deal."

****

Chapter 3

Just One Happy Family?

Out in the sunshine, Alexander dragged a wooden panel on which was painted an ornate column partly covered by a lush velvet green curtain.

"What about a backdrop like this? Something grand an' stately?"

"The green would match my dress," Sarah noted, but Rob shook his head. "Color photography wasn't invented yet. Besides, I want something that looks more like the Civil War."

"Ah, I've just the thing, then." Alexander pulled out another backdrop with a different scene painted on it. Birds rested in the branches of tall majestic trees surrounding a wooded clearing. Faintly in the background, one could just barely see the white tents of soldiers. "An' it'll cost you five dollars less than the ballroom scene."

Jamie peered at the panel. "Those must be Confederate army tents. I see a Rebel flag."

"Oh, who cares?" snapped Sarah. Her voice suddenly sweetened. "It will show off your uniforms so nicely."

Sarah began fussing with her hair in front of a large mirror propped outside the tent, dabbing perfume behind her ears from a small flacon she pulled from her tiny beaded bag.

Alexander pulled the brothers inside for a minute.

"I'm hatin' to be miserly, but I must insist on a deposit of 50 percent. That would be fifteen dollars for the one portrait."

Rob started to haggle, but Jamie fished out three crisp five dollar bills from his black-tarred haversack bag. Alexander stared at one of the five dollar bills.

"Not a good likeness of Mr. Lincoln, is it now? It shows every wrinkle, every blemish, and none of the man's sense of fun an' mischief. Even Robert finally admitted my pictures—I mean, other photographs taken—were far superior to those later done by Mathew Brady's man, that Anthony Berger fellow. And Robert's so fussy, y'know."

"Robert who?" asked Rob.

Alexander gave him a surprised look. "Why, Robert Lincoln, the president's eldest son, of course!"

"Of course," Rob said, acting nonchalant, but nevertheless giving the man a sidelong glance. The guy was weird. Acting as if he'd had conversations with Lincoln's son who would have to be about 150 years old by now!

Alexander pushed the brothers outside the tent. "Now, let's put the lady in the middle." He ducked his head under the camera's black cloth and viewed the scene in his image finder, then popped out again. "An' what a beautiful broach you're wearing, lass!" He walked back to her and examined the ornately decorated pin she wore on her dress. "It looks so old!"

Sarah pulled it away from her dress material so he could see it better. "It's more than one hundred thirty years old, and may have been worn by the wife of a Union officer. I bought it at an antique store near Sharpsburg."

Alexander nodded, impressed. Then he was all business again. "Right, then. The Union man on the lady's left and the Confederate man on her right." He moved them around like chess pieces under the midday sunlight. "No, let's try the lady on the right and the two young men next to each other." He positioned a tree stump. "No, how about the lady seated on this tree stump and one gentleman standing on either side. Now you each put an arm along her back." Back and forth he went, between his subjects and the camera, peering into the camera, adjusting the focus, and then back to his subjects again. Finally, he was satisfied. But Rob wasn't—he wanted to slap Jamie's hand! He couldn't stand to see his brother's dirty hand touching her fine satin dress.

"You must excuse me for two minutes while I sensitize the plate. Do not move even an inch!" He wagged a finger at them. "Remember. . . do not disturb me. I must have total darkness." He disappeared into the inner tent, drawing the curtains tightly behind him.

"Don't you touch her," Rob muttered between clenched teeth. "I'm not touching her, I'm touching her dress," retorted Jamie. "Besides, that's how the Alexander dude posed me."

"I can see what you're doing. You're massaging her shoulder!"

Sarah exploded, without moving a single muscle. "Would you two just . . . shut . . . up?"

A tense silence followed which felt far longer than two minutes. Finally, Alexander emerged from the inner tent, clutching a wooden lightproof container in which the glass plate was securely enclosed. He rushed to insert it into the back of the camera.

"Now, my patient and kind lady and gentlemen, can you hold yourselves perfectly still for at least fifteen seconds?"

A fly buzzed under Rob's nose and he impatiently brushed it away.

"Hmmm, I sense our Rebel might be havin' a problem with that. One moment, please."

Alexander dragged out from the tent what looked like a tall metal stand with a two-pronged clamp on the top. Then he clamped Rob's head, one prong on each side. "My 'immobilizer.' I have to use it on some. But you won't even see it in the picture," he promised.

Jamie laughed. "Yeah, it'll just look like his usual devil horns."

Rob silently seethed.

"All right now, are we ready?" The three tried to nod without moving their heads. "My, my, Johnny Reb. What angry eyes we have today! Oh, well, now dunna move until I stop me hummin'. Dunna even breathe!"

Alexander removed the lens cap, then pulled out an antique watch on a chain which he stared at as he hummed the chorus of "The Battle Hymn of the Republic." Rob could hear his brother snort back laughter. Rob did not dare to move his eyes from the camera, but he could sense his brother caressing Sarah with his fingers again. He would kill him! It was the longest fifteen seconds he had ever experienced.

The humming stopped. Rob reached for his brother. "Why, you little . . . "

But Rob couldn't quite reach him. He had forgotten that his head was clamped.

****

Alexander gave the trio a beady-eyed stare. "You'll have to give me a few minutes to see how the negative turns out. If you made even the slightest movement, or the sunlight is insufficient, your image will be blurred and we will have to do it all over again."

Jamie offered his arm to Sarah. "That's all right. The lady and I are going out to lunch. Mr. 'Hard-core' here can stay and wait for the picture." He turned to Rob. "We're getting hamburgers. Delicious, juicy, McDonald's kind of hamburgers. I'll see if they have any hardtack for you."

Sarah gave Rob a quizzical glance, then walked off with Jamie, her arm linked in his. Rob bit his lip. Had Sarah wanted him to say something? Or had she wanted to go with Jamie? Well, it was too late now.

Alexander gave Rob a sympathetic look. "Yanks getting you down, are they? Come on, lad, I'll give you a little refreshment while we wait for the image to fix. Just give me a few seconds."

Alexander removed the wood-covered glass plate from the camera, then disappeared into the black inner tent. Soon he emerged to escort Rob outside to the front of his main tent, where he reached into an ice bucket, exclaiming, "Ah, nothing like a nice refreshin' ginger beer, is there now?"

Alexander's eyes glinted as he handed Rob a bottle. "So you want to live in the past, do you? 'Twasn't all peaches and cream, you know. Those were hard times, lad."

Rob stared after his brother arm in arm with the girl of his dreams. They dawdled in front of a nearby tent, looking like the perfect old-fashioned couple in the crowd of reenactors.

Rob sighed, as he sipped. "I know, I know. It's just life in modern times isn't so fun, either." He tried to steer the subject away from his own problems. "Well, look at yourself. Wouldn't you like to have been around back then? Be like Mathew Brady and be the first to take photographs of modern warfare?"

Alexander glared at him. "What do you mean, be like Mathew Brady? He was not the first to photograph the war!"

Rob was taken aback. " 'Brady's Album Gallery.' That's what all those famous Civil War photographs say on them."

"And you believe that malarkey, do you?" Alexander jumped up, furious. "Those credits are phony as a three dollar bill! Why, old Mathew was nearly blind as a bat by the time of Antietam! As far as I know, he ne'er went near a battlefield!"

"Then who took all those pictures?" asked Rob, confused.

"Why, his assistants, of course!" The man had truly worked himself into a fury now. "His brilliant, under-paid, overworked assistants!"

"Okay, okay, I believe you." Rob craned his neck, but he had lost sight of the couple. "Is it time to check the negative yet?"

Alexander took a deep breath as if to calm him-self, then gave Rob a sympathetic look. "Just a few more minutes. You watch over my store, lad, while I get you a little snack. I know where to get some fine hardtack." He nodded toward the rear of the tent. "Keep an eye on the rear, too. I've a back entrance and I dunna want trespassers."

He patted Rob on the arm. "Cheer up, lad, I know how it feels to be unappreciated. But your day will come."

Rob sat in front of the tent, lost in thought. Every-thing always came so easily to Jamie. Now it was be-ginning to look like he would get Sarah too. He always got the girls. Who could resist his slow, easygoing charm and his fair good looks?

Rob heard a rustling sound from inside the tent. He stood and cocked his head. Had someone snuck in from the back? He caught a familiar whiff of sunflowers. Then he recognized low musical laughter and the sweet throaty voice he heard in his dreams each night.

"That's enough! Stop it, I said!"

Next he recognized another voice, a hoarse one, much less dear to him.

"Just one kiss, Sarah. One little kiss?"

Rob jumped to his feet and ran into Alexander's tent. Tossed carelessly on the couch was a drum and a familiar black-tarred haversack. He picked up the bag, then with a quiet fury pulled back the inner tent's curtain, the one with the sign that said "NO TRESPASSING."

Rob could not see for a minute, for it was dark inside the tent except for a faint red light which glowed unnaturally.

"R . . . Rob? Is that you?"

Directed by the voice, Rob threw the haversack straight at his brother, who caught it, then attempted to use it as a shield.

Anger flaring inside him, Rob moved toward his brother. "I'm going to kill you!"

Sarah tried to get between the two boys. "Stop it, Rob. I can take care of myself."

Rob punched Jamie squarely on the jaw. But just after he did, his arm knocked against a table and hit a tub full of chemicals. Rob jumped back to avoid the spilling liquid, as the glass plate hit the ground with a thud. The air grew pungent with the sharp smell of acid. Smoke swirled around them.

"What have you done? You've ruined the picture!" cried Sarah. She inhaled sharply. "That smell! It's . . . it's making me dizzy! I . . . I feel faint."

Rob tried to catch her, but he began to feel dizzy too, the dark tent twirling around him. Starting to fall, he braced himself against the table. As he did so, he noticed the glass plate negative on the floor. By the faint red light, he could see the glass had a deep crack down the middle. He could also see three ghostlike figures gradually emerge onto the plate. A beautiful young hoop-skirted lady sitting on a tree stump, with two Civil War soldiers standing on either side of her—the tall one in the Union army's uniform, the shorter one dressed like a Rebel. It looked like the two soldiers wanted to kill each other.

****

Chapter 4

Captured!

"Geez, man!" Jamie held his jaw and shook his head. "You must have knocked me out cold! Where are we?"

Jamie looked around him, confused. He was in a wooded clearing, surrounded by bushes and trees, very much like the backdrop in the picture.

Rob staggered toward Sarah as if dizzy, shielding his eyes from the harsh glare of the sun. "Sarah? Are you all right?"

Sarah nodded, getting up from the tree stump on which she'd been sitting. "What happened? Last thing I remember was being in that tent. I must have fainted."

"Maybe I passed out, too. But what are we doing here?" said Rob.

"Well . . . ," said Sarah, "I don't know how I got here, but I know I'm going back to the camp. I don't want to miss the rest of the reenactment. Bye!" She turned away from the boys and began walking briskly through the woods. Rob ran after her and grabbed at her sleeve.

"No, Sarah, wait! What if we're lost or something?"

"I can see the tents from here, you ninny! Now let me go!" Rob continued to hold onto her sleeve, even as she pulled away from him. RI-I-I-P went the delicate silk material as Rob was left holding only a sleeve.

Jamie couldn't hold back his laughter.

Sarah's eyes flashed with anger. "It's so funny, is it? Well, I'm sending you two my dressmaker's bill! Do you know how many nights I had to babysit to pay for having this old-fashioned dress made?"

Stomping off in the direction of the tents, her head held high, she proceeded to trip over a rock and fall headlong into mud.

Jamie rushed over to help her up and brush her off, only succeeding in making himself almost as muddy as she was. She shook herself free and glared at him. "You . . . animal! Don't you ever . . . ever . . . touch me again!"

She flounced off, trying to make as dignified an exit as her torn and filthy costume and her mud-smeared face would allow.

"She seems sort of mad at me. I really thought she wanted a kiss." Jamie shrugged his shoulders. "Women . . . go figure."

"Jamie, we have bigger problems than your love life here. Like where we are, for instance."

Jamie got up on the tree stump to better survey the surrounding area. "Well, the reenactors' camp is over there where Sarah's going."

Rob jumped onto the stump next to his brother. "Oh, really? Then where is the parking lot?"

Jamie scratched his head, puzzled. "I don't know. It's over there somewhere. Funny, though, I don't see a single car."

Rob looked around the still woods with a rapt expression on his face. "I don't know, Jamie. Everything seems so pristine, so . . . pure. It looks just the way it must have back during the Civil War."

"Come on," said Jamie. "Woods are woods."

"No, really," insisted Rob. "Something feels different. Do you suppose that tent somehow carried us back into the past?"

Jamie shook his brother. "All that hardtack you eat has weighed down your brain, man! We just got lost. Now chill out!"

Jamie reached into his haversack and pulled out his headphones. He would turn to a jazz station. Music was his haven. When things got bad, it always made him feel better.

But he soon took off the headphones, a puzzled look on his face. "That's weird, man. I had it set on radio. But I can't seem to pick up any frequencies. This thing's dead as a doornail."

"Gee, how horrible! I guess you'll have to make do with one of your cassette tapes," said Rob, his voice dripping with sarcasm.

Just then, Rob's eye caught the silvery glint of a saber lying on the ground near the bushes. He walked over and picked it up to examine it.

"Look at this saber! This is an original Civil War piece! Just look at the insignia on this."

"Who cares about stupid weapons?" said Jamie. "Let's just figure out what we're doing here!"

Just then, they heard a nasal voice singing off-key from behind the bushes. "Aa-ah-maaa-zin' Gra--ace, Ho-oww sweeeet the sound . . . "

The bushes parted and a man in a dirty gray uniform emerged, buttoning up the fly of his pants. He was broad-faced with a wide majestic brow and a full beard and moustache, wearing a faded gray forage cap with its brim pulled down almost to his nose.

He stopped short as he noticed Jamie.

"A Yank so near our camp?" Sucking on what appeared to be a lemon, he raised the brim of his cap and stared at the boys with the cold hard eyes of a fanatic. He reached towards Rob and, with a stern Southern accent, said, "My saber! My saber . . . or a court-martial is in order."

They stared at the man with the rigid martial stance. Though the uniform was soiled, dull gold braid was just faintly visible on the sleeves. Darn, thought Jamie, the face looked so familiar!

Turning to Rob, he barked: "Name, company, and regiment, soldier!"

Rob's mouth dropped open. "I got it! You look just like General Stonewall Jackson!"

The man's stern face softened ever so slightly as he continued sucking on his lemon. "Well, of course I do. I *am* General Jackson. Now be a good boy and give me back my saber."

Jamie burst out laughing. "Don't tell me. You're his great-great grandson, right?"

Jackson gave Jamie an odd look, then gave Rob's apparel an appreciative once-over. "That's a fine lookin' uniform you're wearing, soldier. New bootees, too! But I asked you a question, son." His fierce blue eyes blazed directly at Rob. "Your name, company, and regiment?"

Something about the man compelled a response.

"I . . . I'm a new recruit, sir," Rob stammered. "Robert Henry from R . . . Rockville, Maryland. Just joined 21st Virginia, Company B."

Jamie shook his head in disgust. "Cut it out, guys," he said. Rob was only encouraging this lunatic by continuing to play these reenactor games.

Jackson's eyes lit up. "A paleface? Well-done, by God, well-done! General Lee predicted we'd pick up

25,000 Maryland recruits and I hadn't seen a single one till now! Matter of fact, all I've noticed since we crossed the river into Maryland are deserters—by the thousands!" He turned his sharp gaze on Jamie. "Got yourself a Yank bushwhacker, have you?"

Rob pointed the sword at Jamie and gave him a little jab. "Yes, sir!"

Jamie jerked away from the sword. "Hey, lighten up, man! You're hurting me! That's like a real weapon!"

"Of course it's real. Though I'll be the first to admit it's far from useful in real fighting." Jackson held out his hand. "Give it back to me, son, or you'll be in trouble."

Rob handed over the sword, muttering, "Sorry, General."

Jamie groaned. Why were they playing these ridiculous games? They should be getting back to the reenactment. He hoped Sarah had cooled off by now.

Now it was Jackson's turn to point the sword at Jamie. "Yanks seem to be getting younger by the day! How old are you, boy?"

"A lot younger than you are, dude! You're too old for these games. Get a life!"

Rob snatched up a long stick from the ground and jabbed it at Jamie's back. "He's an insolent boy. A yellow-bellied deserter I found lurking in the woods. I left my musket in camp so I had to use this stick here."

Jamie shot his brother an aggrieved look. "Hey, stop with the games, man. You're hurting me!"

Jackson's posture became even more rigid. "Always carry your weapon, private. I've court-martialled men for less." He suddenly remembered his own lapse and blushed. "Except when you're answering the call of nature, that is."

Rob jabbed his brother again until Jamie gave a yelp of pain.

"Cut it out!" cried Jamie. Rob was really starting to make him mad.

"I like your spirit, Henry. You remind me of myself as a boy." He sucked in his breath, then spat out the piece of lemon he'd been chewing. "Aids in digestion," he explained. Then he turned his steely gaze on Jamie. "Well, now, a cowardly Yankee deserter. Perhaps my least favorite kind of Yankee."

He gestured in the direction of the tents. "Son, take the young devil into camp." He peered at Rob. "You're a young one, too, aren't you? You sure you're old enough to muster in, son?"

"Sixteen, sir. I'm a little small for my age."

"Only sixteen? Well, we can scarcely afford to be choosy. We've lost more than 10,000 men since we crossed the river from Virginia." He looked down at Rob's shoes again. "Of course General Lee excused all the ones lackin' shoes."

He aimed his sword at Jamie. "Have you searched the Federal properly and made sure he's without arms?"

Rob pushed his brother against a tree and none too gently began searching him.

Jackson nodded. "I like to see a soldier with some vinegar in him."

"No weapons on him, sir," said Rob, giving him a smart salute. "Excuse me for asking, sir," added Rob. "But if you're really General Jackson, what are you doing walking around the woods by yourself? I mean, shouldn't you be leading troops or something?"

The erect man slumped a bit, massaging his lower back with one hand. "Old quinine told me to walk at least twenty minutes a day to exercise my back. Ever since my new mare threw me it's been ailing me. Think I'll poke around these woods some more and see if I can't find my Little Sorrel."

His posture once again became erect.

"March the prisoner back to the provost guard. We'll see who he is and what he knows. Could be a Lincoln spy!"

Rob saluted. "Yes, sir. Umm . . . where is the provost guard, sir?"

"Why, the tent with the big flag near that red woodshed, where we lock up camp critters, of course. You being such a fresh fish, I allow as you didn't know that."

He tossed Rob his sword. "Here, I'll lend you my sword. See you back in camp, Henry. Full chisel now!" He stood watching with approval as Rob, point of sword in Jamie's back, began marching him in the direction of the campsite.

"Henry!"

Rob stopped short, one hand grabbing Jamie's arm. "Sir?"

"Take the Yank's bootees off. He won't need them where he's headed."

****

Jamie marched in his stocking feet through the woods, his brother poking at his back with the point of the sword. He could feel the needles of pine pricking his feet, and he stumbled over rocks as he turned his head back to yell at his captor.

"I'll get you back for this, you little runt! Wait till I tell Mom!"

Rob ignored him, continuing to prod him forward with the sword, a look of grim determination on his face that sent a chill up Jamie's spine. Was Rob losing his sense of reality? All these war games he took so seriously had finally sent him over the deep end!

The woods soon gave way to a large campsite dotted with row upon row of white canvas tents. Jamie stopped, taking in the smell of frying pork fat, the smoke of countless campfires and the noise of a thousand men preparing a meal.

"I don't remember us having so many Rebel reenactors, do you, Rob?"

Rob laughed unpleasantly. "You still think you're at a reenactment, don't you, dummy?"

As Rob continued to push Jamie through camp, a hush fell over each group of soldiers they passed.

"HISSSSS."

At first Jamie thought he was imagining it. But the sound grew louder and louder. These Rebel reenactor guys were taking their parts far too seriously and Jamie felt increasingly ill at ease. He desperately tried to think of something that would make them laugh, his usual way of coping with trouble.

"HISSSSS." The hissing continued to grow until it was like a tidal wave about to drown him.

Jamie sniffed the air. "Bacon again? Got some lettuce and tomato, so we can have BLT's at least? Make mine on whole wheat. Lightly toasted, please, with plenty of mayo!"

He walked past a group of baseball players who stopped their game and turned to stare at him. "Hey, batter up!" called Jamie. "Who's on second?"

The batter, a man whose tattered flannel shirt strained over his bulging muscles, grabbed Jamie by the arm and shook the fence rail he'd been using as a bat right in Jamie's face.

"A bluebelly! Ah jest hate bluebellies!"

Jamie turned his face away, appalled by the man's stench.

"Phew! You hard-cores go too far! I don't care how dirty the Rebels were supposed to be, you still got to take an occasional bath."

Offended, the man gave Jamie a shove so hard that it landed him against a tree. The man moved toward Jamie, an evil smile lighting up his face as he looked him over. "This bluebird talks too much. But he sure has some nice-lookin' blues on his back. Look newly issued, don't they now? Let's see his shirt." He roughly peeled off Jamie's jacket and shirt, and started to try them on. "Hey, Pitcher, this jacket's too tight for me, think you can wear it?"

The pitcher, tossing the yarn-wrapped walnut he used as a ball, walked over and grabbed the jacket. "How do I look in blue, Lucas?" he chortled.

The first baseman ran over, pulled off Jamie's cap and modeled it for the others. "How 'bout me? Like my new hat?"

"Hey, guys, give it back!" Jamie reached for his cap, but the man pulled it away from him, laughing.

Soon the barefoot second baseman joined them, pushing Jamie to the ground and pulling off his socks. "Nice wool," he said. "Thanks, Yank."

"Hey, Red, how 'bout your belt?" The third baseman yanked off Jamie's belt with the "U.S." brass plate on it. "I'd trade ya, but ya can see I ain't got no belt to give ya in return." He laughed uproariously as he showed how loose his pants were. "Must be all that rich southern food we git. Ya'all think I can file away the 'U' in U.S.A. and change it to a Confederate 'C'?"

The others joined in the laughter, then the big one they called Lucas stopped the merriment. "Hey, wait jest a minute. Gimme that belt. Ah'm tired of playin' rounders. Let's hang us a bluebelly 'fore we eat."

A crowd of foul-smelling Rebels crowded around Jamie, now barefoot and clad only in trousers. They yanked him to his feet and then backed him against the tree. Lucas put the belt around Jamie's neck and fastened it tightly. Jamie looked around desperately for his brother.

"Help!"

There he was, at the back of the crowd! Rob had been watching the whole time! But now, to his relief, Jamie saw him pushing his way through the crowd, brandishing Jackson's sword.

Rob cleared his throat. "There'll be no lynchings today, men." He was using his deep historian's voice. "I'm under orders to take him to the provost."

"Says who?" said Lucas, angry at having his fun interrupted.

"My orders are from Stonewall himself. You see this sword?" Rob waved it dramatically. "It belongs to the General. He wants to question the boy himself. And you know how quick he is to court-martial!"

The pitcher threw his walnut ball high up in the air, then reluctantly gave Jamie his blue jacket back. "Hey, I didn't want to get shot by my own men, nohow." Lucas tossed Jamie his worn, stinking flannel shirt. "I'm only tradin' with ya, bluebelly. I'm givin' ya mine, see?" And slowly, regretfully, the group drifted back to their baseball game.

Jamie threw the man's shirt away from him in disgust, then hurriedly buttoned up his jacket before anyone could have a change of heart. But he was now shirtless, beltless, hatless, and barefoot. "Geez, Rob," he whispered. "Those guys weren't playing games! They were for real. Who were they? And where the heck are we?" He grabbed onto Rob's shoulders and there was fear written in his eyes as the truth dawned on him. "Rob? We're really back in the Civil War days, aren't we?"

In response, Rob just smiled, one of his rare big, broad smiles, as if he had known that all along, and he pushed his brother toward a large, flag-bedecked tent—the tent next to the woodshed.

****

Chapter 5

The Laundry Lady

"There ya are! You'd be the new girl, am I right? I'm Peg O'Brien, regimental vivandiere."

Sarah gasped in surprise as a plump woman wearing a straw hat, a short cotton dress covered by an apron, wool pantaloons sticking out, pulled her out of the woods' edge and pushed her toward a tent.

"Now get out of those dirty old clothes and put on somethin' more presentable. Lord knows, I thought you'd never arrive. Got lost, did you, dearie? Ever since my Mary left, I've been so shorthanded. The officers are goin' plum crazy. They're desperate for clean clothes, I tell you. Now skedaddle! Change your clothes right away, then I'll give you some rations to nibble."

She was such a pushy woman and Sarah felt so disgustingly filthy in her mud-caked clothes that she obeyed, closing the tent's flaps tightly behind her. She peeled off her dirty torn dress, once her pride and joy, and pulled on a plain cotton, loose-fitting, ankle-length frock. As she did so, she wondered who this Peg was and what on earth she had meant by calling Sarah "the new girl." Sarah's stomach growled. Whoever she was, it felt good to get out of her wet dirty clothes and the promise of a snack was tempting. For Sarah suddenly remembered she had left her beaded bag back in the photographer's tent and had no money with which to buy food.

Peg briskly entered the tent. "Well, good enough, good enough, dearie. Though of course you'll be wantin' an apron when you start work."

"Work?" asked Sarah. What on earth was the woman jabbering about?

Peg winked. "Oh, ya city girls! Always jokin'!" She pulled a camp chair over to a table. "Hungry?"

Sarah nodded her head and the woman pushed a tin plate toward her. On it was a slab of pork fat and a biscuit cracker about three inches square and half an inch thick. Sarah looked at the cracker suspiciously, for she could detect tiny black specks moving across its bumpy surface.

"Well, grab a root, dearie, and don't be shy! 'Tis a wonder we have any food at all. Many a day our men's been livin' off green apples and corn plucked fresh from the trees and fields. And you can well imagine what that's been doin' to their poor insides!"

Noticing Sarah eyeing the cracker, Peg brushed it off with her hand. "Oh, a few little weevils is all, dearie. Wouldn't hurt you a bit to get extra nourishment."

Squeezing her eyes shut, Sarah bit into the biscuit and almost broke a filling.

Peg laughed. "Well, why do you think they call it *hard* tack? You city girls certainly are peculiar! Want some Jeff Davis coffee?" From a kettle, she filled up a large tin cup with some greasy black liquid.

Sarah took a gulp, then almost spit it out. "I thought you said coffee."

"I said Jeff Davis coffee, girl. Had to use wheat and chicory this mornin'. Lord knows, we haven't had real coffee for many a day."

Sarah took a tentative poke at the pork fat. "Cholesterol city! Do you eat this stuff often?" Looking at her chubby hostess, Sarah realized that wasn't the most tactful thing to say.

"I don't know what you be jabberin' about. You Frederick girls have a most peculiar accent. Still, I'm thankful your momma sent you to help support the Southern cause. It's nice to know there are a few friendly faces in Frederick town, after all." She lowered her voice confidentially as if someone might be listening outside of the tent. "I promise you you'll make some real coin, dearie, not just Confederate shucks, if you play your cards right."

"Frederick? I'm not from Frederick, I'm from—"

The woman interrupted impatiently. "Now listen, dearie, I've not the time to be hearin' your life's history. Now eat up your vittles. We've no time to lose. Old Stonewall and his aides will be needin' some fresh shirts and under things if they be breakin' camp tomorrow." She pointed to a Confederate uniform hanging from a peg on the tent wall. "And I promised young Kyd Douglas that I'd brush up his uniform as well."

She nudged Sarah and winked. "That Douglas lad is Stonewall's aide, a local boy, I hear tell. And he's quite young and handsome, though a bit on the smallish side."

She waddled over to a calendar, hanging next to the uniform, repeating: "They'll be breakin' camp tomorrow, so I heard."

Sarah looked over where the woman's chubby finger pointed. Her hands were red, rough and peeling; the nails were broken off and chipped. Talk about your dishpan hands! Sarah pretended to chew on the piece of fat, but surreptitiously spit it into her hand. Then she glanced over at the calendar Peg was pointing at, featuring paintings of lush green countryside.

Sarah did a double take. For Peg's fat finger pointed at today's date marked "Tuesday, September

9" and at the top of the picture—in bold writing, as clear as could be—"September, 1862."

Sarah quickly recovered. This reenactor was almost as bad as Rob in the extremes to which she would go. "Where did you get the calendar?" Sarah asked. "It looks so authentic."

Peg gave Sarah a strange look. "Well, I'm not sure what 'authentic' be meanin,' but me dear friend back in Galway County sends me a new one each year. I may be just a war widow scrapin' to get by, but I still like to keep current with the fashions, y'know."

Looking at her worn red hands, her lank greasy hair pulled back in a bun, and her sturdy men's work boots, Sarah struggled not to laugh.

"Come on, girl, you'll have to work for your supper, you will!"

Before Sarah could protest, the woman had put an apron on her, pinning the top white bib across her chest, and dragged her over by a smoky fire.

There were several large cast-iron pots of water supported over the fire by a metal tripod—the pots filled with various shirts and handkerchiefs and under clothing submerged in bubbling soapy water. Peg tossed some handfuls of wood ash into the pots, grabbed up a long wooden paddle and gave the clothes a twirl.

"Just keep stirrin' those pots now. For about two hours, then I'll come back and help you drain it all down and fill it up again. I'll be back in the camp collectin' more of the officers' shirts to wash. The soldier boys can do their own." She cheerfully held her nose. "Not that they do it regular, mind you."

Sarah stared at her, uncomprehending.

"But . . . but . . . I just came to watch the battle."

"Lord have mercy, my girl, war's no game or I would not be a poor widow havin' to work like this. Battles aren't like shows you can watch while eatin' your picnic supper." She gave a bitter laugh. "I think the fine ladies and gents of Washington learned that at Manassas, they did, when real gunfire began soilin' their fine clothes an' spoilin' their fun picnic outing!"

I'm getting out of here, thought Sarah. This woman was nuts! She made a motion to leave, but Peg stopped her. "And you cannot just go traipsin' around camp with all the men folk here, dearie." She gave her a wink. "Unless you're wearin' man's clothing, that is. And between you and me, I'd wager there are several girls doin' just that kind of play acting right here in this camp."

Peg handed her the paddle. "Now get down to work, Sarah dear. The logs are over there if the fire starts to die. Keep that water boilin' to kill off all the graybacks."

"Graybacks?" asked Sarah.

"You know . . . the lice. Camp's swarmin' with 'em."

Sarah shuddered. With a wave of her hand, Peg waddled off.

****

Sarah stirred the clothes thoughtfully. Something felt very wrong. This laundry lady did not seem to be play acting, and, as she looked around at the outskirts of the camp, this did not look like the reenactment grounds.

She tried to recall the sequence of events which had led her to this predicament. It was all Jamie's fault—convincing her to sneak back into that photographer's tent by the back entrance. She remembered being in the little darkroom tent when Jamie tried to kiss her. The truth was, she now admitted, she was attracted to him. If only he were a little smarter, less immature, more serious . . . like Rob, she realized with a start. If only she could combine the two boys into one man, for each possessed qualities she liked but was lacking in others.

Thinking about Rob made her recall the fight in the darkroom, that awful acid smell when the tub fell over, and the way the tent had seemed to twirl around and around her before she fainted and then wound up seated on the stump in the forest. In the very position in which she had posed for the photograph! She remembered how strange and secretive that photographer Alexander G. had been. How nervous he had seemed about the thought of anyone entering the darkroom tent! Was there something magical about that tent? Had it somehow moved them to the past?

Worrying about all these things made Sarah feel she would lose her mind. She was sorry now that she had lost her temper and separated from Rob and Jamie back in the woods. She had to find them! Together, they would figure out what was going on. She squinted into the distance to see more of the camp. They had to be around here someplace.

Several Rebel soldiers walked by. She started to say hi, but seeing their hard-looking eyes staring at her made her hold her tongue. She looked down at the barrel of suds, avoiding eye contact. They looked like the real thing, all right, young, but lean and hungry like wolves, not your usual well-fed, weekend reenactor types. She seemed to be the only girl around and she felt increasingly uneasy about that. Yet she had to search the camp to see if she could find the Henry brothers.

She stabbed with annoyance at the smelly clothes rising to the surface of the bubbling water and tried to skim away some of the scum. Sarah Singleton, working as a laundry lady, indeed! She had to get away from this ridiculous job. If only there were some way she could make herself less conspicuous . . . .

Suddenly, Sarah remembered something she'd seen hanging in Peg's tent. Something just about her size.

****

Chapter 6

Jeff Davis Coffee Strikes Again

WEDNESDAY, SEPTEMBER 10, 1862

Early morning sunlight peeked through the slats of the woodshed and woke Jamie up to another day of captivity. Jamie scratched a second line in the dirt floor of the shed. He must keep a hold on reality, and counting the days was a way to do that. Luckily, no one had discovered his Sony Walkman yet. Now he understood why he couldn't listen to the radio—it hadn't been invented!

Jamie began to play the only tape he had with him, snapping his fingers to the beat of the music. It was a good thing he was a lazy guy by nature. If this had been Rob holed up in a shed, with no fresh air or exercise, he would have gone crazy by now. The food was pretty bad, of course, and sleeping in a lice-ridden blanket was far from fun—but, well, he was alive, wasn't he?

Jamie scratched at his back and legs. Truth be told, living in the Civil War was no picnic. This would teach Rob to stop romanticizing about the good ol' days! Still, Rob was probably thriving as a Confederate soldier, while Jamie suffered as a prisoner.

And—this was the thought that most scared Jamie—when they left camp (and even through the shed door, he could sense the Rebel troops were preparing to move out, what with all the noises of barrels rolling, horses neighing and wagons moving), what if they shipped him off to one of those infamous, disease-ridden camps for prisoners of war! Rob had once shown him photographs of prisoners who came out of those camps at the war's end, and they resembled the walking dead who had emerged from Nazi concentration camps, looking more like skeletons than people.

In a brief interview with Stonewall Jackson last night, the General had assured him that if the prisoner exchange agreement worked out, he could be traded within days for a Confederate prisoner of equal rank. That sounded fine in theory, but Jamie realized that the name of James Henry—the twentieth century reenactor drummer boy who wasn't even a legitimate member of a regular reenactor unit, much less the real thing—would hardly be on the Yankee roster of soldiers missing in action. And if the Union bureaucracy claimed no knowledge of him, his chances of being shipped to one of those death camps would increase considerably.

Escape—he had to figure out a way to escape! But coming up with clever plans had never been his strong suit. That was Rob's strength. Jamie was the charmer, and he couldn't see how all his skills at making friends could get him out of this pickle.

Charming girls, now that had really been his strong point. He thought about those moments in the photographer's tent, kissing Sarah Singleton. Man, that had almost been worth all this trouble! For though she had protested, he knew deep inside that she liked him and suspected she had savored that kiss almost as much as he had.

But then Jamie remembered how she had run away from him in the woods. Where was she now? Was she safe? A rough Rebel army camp was hardly the place for a pretty young girl, even a strong resourceful one like Sarah. She'd be better off on the Union side, he thought. He knew he was near Frederick, Maryland, and that the date was September 10, 1862—he had learned that much from Stonewall Jackson. Now he wished with all his might he had paid more attention to his history lessons. He knew this was about one week before the Battle of Antietam but he couldn't for the life of him remember when the Union forces reached Frederick. Not only for Sarah's sake—for his sake, too—for when the Union forces came, he could be liberated. Unless he were long gone to—POW camp!

Jamie saw a shaft of sunlight widen, as the shed door slowly creaked open. He stuffed his tiny Sony Walkman into the pocket of his pants.

"Slosh time," said a young Rebel guard who prodded him to his feet with a musket.

Jamie stood blinking in the bright morning sun. "Does that mean I get hosed down with water?" asked Jamie hopefully. He could sure use a shower right now. Wash off some of those lice!

The Rebel, wearing an oversized cap shading his eyes, gave Jamie a rough push. "Come on o'er near the fire, Yank, and ya'all will see what you get."

Uh-oh, thought Jamie. What would they do to him by the fire? They didn't brand prisoners, did they?

Much to his relief, his guard plopped down some mushy gruel on a tin plate and thrust it at him. Jamie gave it a curious sniff, then wolfed it down.

"Cornmeal fried in bacon grease, slooshed aroun' with a lot of water. Jest like my Ma used to make," the boy said, and the wistful tone in his voice caught Jamie's interest. Maybe here was someone he could make his ally!

Trying to stall, warming his hands by the fire, he tried to get a conversation going. "How old are you, Johnny Reb? You look to be only about my age."

The boy glanced around the campfire nervously as if to see if anyone could hear them. "Fourteen, Billy Yank, and that's the God-awful truth. Ah lied my way into this soldier's life and now ah'm regrettin' it more and more by the day."

Jamie smiled his warmest smile. "Just about the same age as me, Johnny my man, and I feel about the same way you do. War sure is hell, ain't it?"

The boy looked grim. "Ain't seen the elephant yet an' ah'm startin' to pray I won't. To tell the truth, ain't so sure I'll hold up so well when the muskets start to fire. How's the war treatin' you, Billy?"

"The name is Jamie, my man. And I can't complain. I ain't dead and I ain't in prison camp."

"Not yet, Jamie, not yet," the boy responded, sending a chill through Jamie despite the fire's warmth. The boy thrust a tin cup at him. "Watch out now, it's Jeff Davis coffee, and ya'all might not be used to it."

Grimacing at the bitter brew, Jamie fished around in a pocket for something to give his guard as a token of his appreciation and to further butter him up. His hands touched his last candy Lifesaver in a roll. He offered it to him and the boy's hands closed over his, warming his insides in a most thrilling yet oddly familiar way.

On an impulse, Jamie pushed the boy's cap back and gasped as he saw strands of golden-red hair slip out.

"S . . . Sarah? Is that you?" he croaked.

"Shhhh! Don't say a word," whispered Sarah, then she gave him a wink. "Didn't know how friendly the Rebs could be, did ya'all?"

Jamie took another gulp of the coffee, his mind racing. How could he have been so blind? Now that he looked more closely, he could see the smallish shoulders and the slight swelling of the chest. Could the two of them escape together? There were soldiers everywhere!

She cleared her throat loudly and called out to a nearby group of soldiers. "Takin' the prisoner to the latrine, boys. Be back in jest a few."

Some of the men snickered. "Take your time, boy. That Yank likely has a case of the Tennessee trots."

Another laughed. "Thar delicate li'l bellies don't take kindly to that Jeff Davis coffee, ah hear tell. Now don't bring him back till it's out of his system."

Sarah tied Jamie's hands with rope. "Sorry, Jamie. I know it hurts, but it'll look better if I do it."

Sarah walked him out to the edge of the camp where a shallow, uncovered trench lay dug up near the woods. The smell was foul from the excrement lying the entire length of the trench. Flies swarmed everywhere. Though there were soldiers by the thousands in the distance, for the moment they were alone.

"Untie my hands!" Sarah untied him and he immediately reached for her. "Sarah Singleton, I can't believe it!"

She pulled away from him. "Geez, Jamie, maybe I should tie your hands up again!" She smiled impishly. "Besides, this is not exactly the most romantic spot, is it now? Have you seen Rob?"

"You care more about him than you do about me, don't you?" asked Jamie, his feelings hurt.

"Don't start that again. He's your brother, isn't he?"

"Oh, don't worry about him. I'm sure he's fine. Probably off bonding with his fellow Rebs even as we speak. You know he wouldn't want to leave even if he could. He's died and gone to Reb heaven here."

"The point is," said Sarah, ignoring his remarks. "If that Alexander guy and his photo-developing tent had something to do with getting us back into the past, maybe we can find him again and he can get us back. I mean . . . I know this sounds weird, but maybe he knows how to time travel!"

Jamie looked at her incredulously, wondering why he hadn't thought of that.

Sarah saw some soldiers ambling in their direction. "Quick, act like you're using the latrine!"

Jamie grabbed his stomach. "I don't need to act. That Jeff Davis coffee really is working on me!"

Sarah turned her head away. "Look, this is just a working hypothesis, okay? But if Alexander was from the past, my guess is he was on the Union side. 'Cause I remember the pictures in his tent were mainly pictures of Union soldiers, at least the ones who were alive. Which means he probably hung out with the Army of the Potomac. So we really should get over to the Union side as soon as we can. I prefer them, anyhow."

"Well, don't you think I do? Man, some of those Rebs almost lynched me!" said Jamie. "But how do we get to the Union dudes?"

"Don't you remember the Antietam campaign at all, Jamie? The Army of the Potomac arrived in Frederick only a few days after the Confederates left camp. So as these guys are breaking camp, all we have to do is slip away, hide out in this area for a few days, and wait for the Union army to come marching in. We can mingle with them, find out if they know any photographers who travel with the army."

Jamie looked skeptical. "I don't know how easy it'll be to just mingle with the Union army. I mean, you could just be a local Frederick girl, but me . . . "

"You're wearing a Union army uniform, aren't you?"

Jamie looked down at his uniform, now filthy and missing several items. "That's the point! They might think I'm a deserter and shoot me!"

Sarah laughed. "Oh, Jamie, you're too nice for anyone to shoot! Besides, you'll be bearing gifts guaranteed to double your soldierly charm." She began pulling things out of her various pockets. A bar of laundry soap, a wad of tobacco, a stack of playing cards, a bright red bandanna and the Lifesaver Jamie had just given her. "See all the goodies I've been accumulating while in camp?"

Jamie looked at her with admiration. "I knew there was a reason I loved you. You have brains as well as beauty."

Watching to make sure the soldiers were moving away from them, she drew closer to Jamie and whispered, "Come on, let's slip into the woods now. Maybe Rob's already there." She pulled him behind a clump of trees.

"Oh, who needs Rob, anyhow?" said Jamie. He was feeling good. All he had to do was just slip into the woods with Sarah, a delightful prospect if he ever had one. Maybe they could even find that Alexander dude and get back home again. But even if they couldn't, he'd be alone with Sarah, and wouldn't that be fun!

Startled, he saw Sarah peeling off her clothes. "Wh . . . What are you doing, Sarah?"

"I'm going to be a girl again!" Underneath her uniform was a plain cotton frock. She threw the gray outfit at him. "Quick! Put these on over your Union uniform. You'll blend in better."

Sarah then dropped her musket, jumped over the latrine and slipped into the woods, sliding off her Rebel cap as her long red-gold hair cascaded down her back.

Jamie struggled into the tight-fitting clothes as fast as he could. The trousers were too short and he could barely get them over his hips. But they were the right color!

Then, with a glance around him to make sure no one was near, Jamie dashed after her.

****

Chapter 7

In Frederick Town

Hidden by trees, Jamie and Sarah watched the Rebels depart.

It was an unimpressive parade. Ragged, dirty, smelly, many of the soldiers barefoot, they marched in slipshod fashion, no two dressed the same, their guns carried at varying angles. Townspeople lined the cobblestone streets to watch them leave, but only a few cheered them on their way.

Hand in hand, Jamie and Sarah listened to the fading footsteps and drum rolls, the creaking noise of supply and artillery wagon wheels, and the final shouts of men on the move—and glad of it—as the last of the Rebels marched from the town.

A familiar voice suddenly rang out from behind a bush.

"They wouldn't be so cheery if they knew the Battle of Sharpsburg was only a week away . . . the bloodiest single day in American history."

"Rob!" Sarah dropped Jamie's hand and rushed over. "Thank God, you're all right!"

He was covered with leaves and twigs and as Sarah brushed him off, he basked in her concern.

44

Jamie looked less happy to see him. "Hey, why didn't you march off with your southern pals?"

A guilty look crossed Rob's face. "Oh, I plan to . . . I will . . . just as soon as I take care of some . . . um . . . business."

Sarah's laughter held a slightly hysterical edge. "Some business? Well, yes, I should say so! The business of getting us out of this ridiculous time warp! What happened in that tent, Rob?"

Rob gave them both a fierce look. "That's exactly what I'd like to know. What were you guys doing—kissing in the dark?"

Sarah looked away, embarrassed. "No . . . I mean, what happened that sent us back to the Civil War?"

"That Alexander guy must be some kind of time traveler," Rob said. "I knew something strange was going on when he talked about Robert Lincoln and Mathew Brady as if he knew them personally!"

"So why didn't you warn us, jerk?" asked Jamie.

"Alexander did warn us. He told us not to go in the black tent, and there were warning signs all over it, but you guys went in, anyway!"

"Well, let's not waste time arguing over spilled milk," said the ever-practical Sarah. "Let's go find Alexander and see if he can help us time-travel back. After all," she added, giving both boys a smug look. "I have cheerleading practice on Friday and a date Saturday night."

"Who do you have a date with?" asked Jamie, but Rob's next remark is what really set him off.

With seeming nonchalance, Rob declared: "Hey, I'm in no hurry to find Alexander. I'm glad we're back in the past. Maybe I can improve it in some way. You know, change things."

Sarah gave him a shocked look. "Rob! You wouldn't want the South to win the war, would you? You're not pro-slavery, are you?"

"Not all the Southerners supported slavery. And if people want to separate from a country, why not? Besides, I want to see what it was really like at the Battle of Sharpsburg."

Jamie's mouth dropped open. "Are you crazy, man? You just said it was the bloodiest day in American history, didn't you?"

"I'm not a coward like you are, Jamie. You're afraid of the sight of blood. You used to pass out when we went for shots at the doctor's. You were—"

"Shut up!" yelled Jamie, glancing at Sarah.

"No, you shut up!" retorted Rob.

As they argued back and forth, they continued walking and before they knew it they were out of the wooded area and entering the town of Frederick. With the departure of the Rebel troops, the town was getting back to normal. Carriages drove up the main street, driven by men in long coats wielding buggy whips. Women in hoop skirts and bonnets walked by, often glaring at Jamie and Rob before they entered the shops.

"Man, it's hot wearing two jackets," said Jamie, shrugging off his gray jacket.

The dirty looks at Jamie were replaced by smiles.

"Well," noted Sarah. "I guess this town is pro-Union." Soon, she began looking in the shop windows.

"Ooh, I just love that bonnet!" exclaimed Sarah, starting to make a beeline for one of the shops.

"Wait! Look at *that* bonnet!" exclaimed Jamie, grabbing her arm and pointing to another shop, in front of which he saw a wagon with a black, oversized hood, its horse tethered to a post.

"Come on! That could be our man!"

Jamie and Sarah ran into the shop nearest the buggy. But Rob hung back, watching.

****

A large man with a big head had his back turned to them as he stood at the counter. "An' I want two cases of collodion and of iodide of silver—highest quality— just as soon as you can obtain it. Just add it to our bill of payment."

Jamie nudged Sarah at the sound of the familiar Scottish brogue.

"Hmm. That bill of payment keeps getting longer and longer, Mr. Gardner. Were it not for your employer Mr. Brady's sterling reputation . . . ."

"I plan to start my own gallery," said Alexander in a proud voice.

"Hmm, you'd best pony up then, Mr. Gardner."

"I will honor all my debts. Just as soon as the great battle is over."

"Expecting a big battle, are you? And where would that be occurring?" asked the proprietor.

"Only the Army of the Potomac knows where she be headin'—and I'm not even sure they know."

Laughing heartily at his joke, Alexander Gardner turned around, but as he saw Jamie and Sarah, the laughter died in his throat.

"By God, 'tis me reenactor friends! And where is brother Robbie?"

Jamie pointed outside.

With a brisk nod to the proprietor, Alexander grabbed Jamie and Sarah, an arm around each of them, and hustled them out of the shop. Rob joined them.

"Rob, me lad!" He shook Rob's hand heartily. Clearly, Rob was his favorite, thought Jamie with a pang of jealousy.

"Come, we must talk in private." He scooped them into his peculiar darkroom buggy, then sat himself in the front driver's seat and whipped the horse forward.

"Weirder and weirder," muttered Jamie, looking around in the coach's dark interior. Lining the walls were shelves built right into the wagon, and tightly fitting into the shelves were row upon row of glass plates, wooden plate holders, heavy negative boxes, bottles of chemicals and—in the rear—several tripods and a large stereoscopic camera with twin lenses.

"Well, we know his last name now, at least," said Sarah. "That man in the store called him Gardner."

"Wow! Do you know who he is, then?" whispered Rob, excited.

"Yeah, the one who got us into this time traveling mess," said Jamie, disgusted.

"He's Alexander Gardner— Mathew Brady's right-hand man! He was supposed to have been a genius— knew all about chemistry and physics and astronomy, far ahead of his time!"

"Yeah, well, it'll take a genius to get us out of this mess," said Jamie.

"Oh, quit grumbling, Jamie!" said Sarah. The wagon suddenly halted, and she fell forward into Rob's arms. Rob blushed, as Jamie yanked her up. Alexander's big head peered into the wagon.

"You young 'uns all right? Havin' a wee bit of trouble with my horse, I'm afraid."

They started to get up, but he pushed them back down onto the bench.

"No, let us talk in the wagon. We're a bit outside the town. Ne'ery a soul will disturb us in here."

It was eerie sitting inside the still, dark wagon with the mysterious man from the past and for a moment they just sat there in wonderment.

Until Sarah broke the silence. "What on earth are we doing here, Mr. Alexander Gardner? And can you get us back?"

Alexander shifted uncomfortably. "I must confess, I dunna know for sure. I have been experimentin' with time travel and you must forgive me if I have not worked out all the kinks in it yet." He gave Sarah and Jamie a hard stare. "An' what gave you the right to go pokin' into my darkroom tent when I told you most particularly not to go in there?"

Jamie looked embarrassed, but Sarah spoke up.

"Well, none of your business and it's a free country (at least in the North), but meanwhile you better use that genius brain of yours to figure out how to get us back. Or I'll . . . I'll . . . sue you."

At this threat, Alexander burst into laughter. "You'll sue me, will you? An' how much do you think you could get from me, lass? Do you fathom how much me an' Mathew Brady are in debt for our photographic supplies and all this confounded war travelin'? An' what a strange twentieth century notion, anyhow!" Suddenly he grew serious. "Now listen, lads, were you wearin' something original, something real, from the Battle of Antietam period when I took your picture? I know the lady was. An' I know that can help facilitate the time traveling."

Sarah nervously fingered the broach at her throat.

"My hat," said Rob proudly. "An ancestor of mine wore it at the Battle of Sharpsburg."

They all looked at Jamie.

He shrugged. "Hey, I'm just not into that hardcore reenactor stuff. Mail-order sutler gear is good enough for me."

"But perhaps in the darkroom tent, were you holding onto anything at all that was an original?" probed Alexander.

Rob snapped his fingers. "Your haversack! Remember, I threw it at you? That looked like an original!"

Jamie scratched his head. "I doubt it. I bought it from Dirty Bob's Sutlery."

Rob groaned. "You bought gear from Dirty Bob? You never know where he gets his junk!"

"Yeah, well, he said the haversack was an original, but I didn't believe him." He smacked his head in frustration. "Geez, what a pain! For once in his life, Dirty Bob didn't rip me off!"

"Now listen, lads and lass, have you anything modern and from your contemporary period on your person now? Perhaps that would help us get you back again."

"Well, I refuse to listen to any more of this. I'm staying in this time period. This is where I belong," declared Rob, bursting out of the wagon into the fresh air.

"So who needs him," said Jamie, furious. "Sarah and I can go back without him."

Alexander shook his head. "You have to be in this together, children. You have to duplicate the picture, all of you . . . one happy family, remember?"

Sarah turned to Jamie. "Let me handle this." She patted her disheveled hair in place and put on her most alluring smile. As she started to get out of the wagon, Jamie stopped her, looking grim.

"No, let me do it. He's my brother and I know him better than you do."

As Jamie climbed out of the wagon, a group of little boys suddenly appeared and began pelting Rob with handfuls of mud and apple cores.

"Secesh trash! Eat your hash! Go back down to Dixie!" They chanted, continuing to throw garbage at Rob. Jamie yelled at the boys to stop, and a mud ball hit the carriage horse smack in the flank. The nervous filly reared back and neighed.

Before they could fully grasp what was happening, the photographic buggy, led by the frightened horse, went roaring out of sight. The boys' last image was of Alexander's big burly body scrambling forward from the buggy onto the front seat, trying desperately to control his runaway horse.

Chapter 8

The Lost Dispatch

The boys started running after the carriage, but it soon left them far behind in a cloud of dust. Jamie gave up first; then, more reluctantly, Rob.

"There goes the Alexander dude and our last chance to get out of here!"

Rob glared at him. "And don't forget Sarah was in the wagon too!"

"Man, I hope she'll be okay." Then another thought crossed his mind. "Oh, oh, she better stick with that Alexander dude 'cause he can't get us back unless we're all three together."

Rob glared at him again. "Maybe she'd be better off without him. How do you know what kind of weirdo he is? After all, he is some kind of time traveler." Rob began walking swiftly away from the road towards the woods.

"Where are you going?" asked Jamie, trying to catch up, still out of breath from their chase.

"None of your business," snapped Rob, breaking into a run.

Jamie tried running after him, calling: "Rob! We gotta stick together! It's our only hope of getting back!"

51

But Rob was a strong runner, and he left Jamie far behind.

"Where on earth is he going?" Jamie wondered, racking his brains. He couldn't still be chasing after Alexander and Sarah, he thought, for he's going in the opposite direction.

Jamie started once again to run after his brother, but he soon collapsed, exhausted. He felt his stomach cramp up the way it had in the Rebel camp. He remembered he hadn't eaten anything since that horrible slosh and coffee meal he had had at sunrise. The sun was going down now and Jamie felt very, very tired.

****

"How are you feeling, son?"

The words were spoken with concern, and Jamie blinked his eyes open to see a grandmotherly-looking woman standing over him.

He looked around him, confused. He was in an old feathered bed, high off the floor, covered by a quilt, in a floral wallpapered room. He peeked under the quilt and much to his embarrassment, found himself dressed in only his underwear.

"Now don't have a conniption fit, son. I have plenty of grandchildren I'm used to caring for. I jest thought you wouldn't be too comfortable in that hot woolen uniform you had on. You were a mite feverish and sufferin' from the Tennessee trots, as well. But regular doses of tincture of opium fixed you up jest fine."

"You had me on opium drugs, lady? How long have I been sleeping?"

"Oh, it's been about three days now." She glanced at his uniform hanging on a peg on the wall. "You look too young to be a soldier, anyhow. Now tell me if your stomach feels better."

"Yeah, thanks, lady, it does. It just feels empty."

"It's no wonder you're hollow, boy. Why, all I've given you is water. Pa and I found you by the side of the road, all tuckered out. Now let my grandchild Caroline bring you some fixin's."

Within minutes, a pretty teenaged girl with big brown eyes and dark hair pulled back in a low bun, wearing a full skirt with apron, bustled into the room bearing a tray. She put the tray down on a bedside table; on it was a plate of cornbread and a bowl full of steaming hot chicken broth.

She watched Jamie gobble up the food. "Are you really a Union soldier?" she asked.

Noting the admiration in her eyes, Jamie nodded. "Yeah, sure. I've seen my share of fighting."

"Well, don't you fret none, soldier boy, your comrades in arms is coming into Frederick now." She lowered her voice confidentially. "You know, most of us in this town are partial to the Union. We jest hated it when the Rebs was here."

Jamie remembered his predicament. "What day is today?"

"Saturday."

"What date?"

The girl glanced over at a wall calendar. "September 13."

"What year?" He just had to be sure.

She gave him a strange look. "Eighteen hundred and sixty-two. You are a strange bird. You talk odd too."

"So do you, doll. So do you." He climbed out of bed, forgetting he was only wearing underwear. The girl blushed, then burst into laughter at his strange, modern-looking underpants.

Jamie had never been into dressing with total authenticity. Leave that ridiculous waist-to-ankle flannel underwear for those ultra-reenactors like Rob. Rob! Where was he? And what on earth was he up to? Suddenly, he remembered Rob's words: "Maybe I can make it better than it was. You know, change things."

Jamie looked at the pretty girl. "Caroline, right?"

She nodded, looking pleased he knew her name.

"Do you know the way to the Rebels' old campground?"

"Of course I do. Everyone in town does."

"Would you please take me there, Caroline?" She hesitated, but after he gave her one of his most lovable smiles, she nodded. It was nice to know his charms worked as well on nineteenth-century girls as they did on twentieth-century ones!

****

Jamie jumped out of the wagon, throwing a kiss goodbye to Caroline. "Thanks for the ride, doll!"

He sauntered over to where he had known he would find his brother—on the old Reb camping ground, searching.

"Whatcha lookin' for, bro'?"

Rob looked up, startled. "J. . . Jamie, hi. How are you?"

"As if you care! You ran off and left me without a word. I fell by the side of the road, sick as a dog!"

"Sorry, I didn't realize you were sick. You seem all right now, though."

"Yeah, well, thanks to the women folk of Frederick town. I could have died, though. They say diarrhea killed more men than minie balls did."

"Nothing could kill you off. Unfortunately. And I said I was sorry." Rob dropped down on his belly, searching for something, crawling through the filthy grass still covered with the debris of an army that had left in a hurry. Stray dogs sniffed along the ground with him, pawing through empty flour barrels, discarded packing crates, and picked-clean chicken bones.

Jamie watched his search. "I know what you're looking for."

"Just . . . um . . . a contact lens."

"You're wearing both your contact lenses now, you liar, or you wouldn't be able to see. I know how nearsighted you are."

Rob pretended to squint. "You're right. I can't see a thing." Then he began to sniff the ground like the hounds near him.

Jamie dropped down to the ground too, and caught the faint scent of cigars. "Three cigars, right? Wrapped inside a certain piece of paper? Lost orders dropped from the pocket of some careless Rebel officer?"

"I don't know what you're talking about," said Rob, but suddenly his eyes gleamed. "Aha!" he exclaimed, snatching a thick white envelope from the ground.

"Give it to me! General Lee's 'lost dispatch' is meant to be found by Union soldiers. You know they give it to General McClellan. You cannot tamper with history, Rob!"

"Says who?"

"I do, you Rebel rat!"

The two brothers fought over the envelope, wrestling all over the filthy campground for it. Suddenly, the dogs began barking and Jamie heard the sound of horses and marching infantry.

"Hey, man, you better split! That's the Army of the Potomac coming!"

Rob snatched the envelope back. "Yeah, nice try." Then he froze like a statue, the envelope dropping from his fingertips. Jamie deftly snatched it up. They heard the shout of a command, in a distinctly Northern accent.

"Fall out, men! Stack arms! Then rest."

In marched the troops of the Army of the Potomac.

"See, Rob? I told you!" Jamie whirled around to gloat. But Rob was gone.

****

Chapter 9

Jamie Makes Friends— and Enemies—in High Places

"Who is responsible for bringing me this?" General George B. McClellan waved the thick envelope in the air while pounding his gloved fist on the table. McClellan had been conferring with a group of Frederick businessmen, in addition to the usual officers and hangers-on he attracted, so his headquarters was crowded. But when he asked the question, one after another of the men stepped back, until only Jamie stood there before him.

"Well, sir, it wasn't only me . . . ."

McClellan fixed on him a severe look. "Your name and unit!"

"James Henry, sir, and I used to be a drummer boy with . . . um . . . 16th Connecticut. I got separated from my chums, sir, and was captured by the Rebs. But I escaped. And I must tell you, sir, with all due modesty, that it wasn't just me that found this lost dispatch. You see, several of the men of the 27th Indiana were interested in the cigars. Now, me, I'm not a smoker (can't stand the stuff, actually), so I was more interested in the document."

The little General clapped Jamie on the back so hard he almost fell over. "You found Lee's secret orders? Bully for you, boy! Bully for you!"

Jamie looked down modestly. "Nothing a red-blooded American boy wouldn't do for his country, sir."

"Do you realize what we have in our hands? General Lee's Special Order 191 outlines his entire plan to divide the Confederate army and use three of his units to attack Harper's Ferry! How very careless!" A cautious look came over his face, erasing the previous joy. He bellowed: "Pinkerton!"

Jamie turned to see an average-sized man with extraordinarily well-muscled arms and shoulders almost instantly appear. He was not dressed in a soldier's uniform, but rather in a red checkered shirt, a black bow tie and a debonair derby perched low on his forehead. He had a small round face framed on bottom by a trim black beard. His narrow black eyes grew even smaller when alarmed, as he clearly was now.

"General, please . . . ," he whispered. "As head of the Secret Service, I must employ another name. Please call me Major Allen in public."

Jamie, overhearing this exchange, could not suppress a chuckle. Man, the Secret Service sure was amateur in those days!

"May I help you, General?" asked Pinkerton, a.k.a. Major Allen, louder this time, though first darting Jamie a dirty look.

"Do you think this could be a hoax? Planted by some crafty Rebel?" asked the General anxiously.

Pinkerton slowly and deliberately opened up the envelope, pulled out one of the cigars, examined it, then lit it. He exhaled with obvious satisfaction, then offered one of the remaining two to McClellan. "This is no humbug, General. This is as genuine as this cigar.

I had it checked by one of our division adjutants who just happened to be an old school chum of the Reb's adjutant general who signed it. Recognized his handwriting immediately."

McClellan jumped from his chair, throwing his arms up in excitement. "Now I know what to do! Here is a paper with which, if I cannot whip Bobby Lee, I will be willing to go home!"

Pinkerton looked around nervously. "General, please, there are many people around." He blew some cigar smoke in Jamie's direction. "People whom we know precious little about."

"Let me savor my little moment of victory here. Must you always be so suspicious, . . . um . . . Major Allen?"

"That's what I'm paid for, sir. That's my job." He blew another smoke ring directly at Jamie, causing him to cough and sputter. "And if I were you, sir, I'd keep a close eye on that boy and have me check out his story. He talks too much."

"Yeah, maybe so," shot back Jamie, "but you listen too much. You must have been eavesdropping right outside the door."

Pinkerton moved in closer to him. "And you yourself were eavesdropping when I whispered to the General!" He reached out and began touching Jamie's head in various spots.

Jamie jumped back. "Hey, man, what do you think you're doing?"

"I'm an expert in phrenology. I know a man by the shape and feel of his head." His hands crept back onto Jamie's head. "Hmm . . . makes friends easily. Too easily! A flatterer. Insincere. Untrustworthy. Immature. Cowardly!"

"I resent that!" said Jamie, stung, moving away from him.

"I know what you are!" said Pinkerton. "I'll bet you're one of those yellow-bellied bounty jumpers. You join the army just long enough to get your $300 bonus, then pooph! You vanish into thin air right before the battle starts. Then you join another unit and pick up another $300 enlistment bonus." He jabbed Jamie with the butt of his cigar. "I know your type. I'll wager you never even seen the elephant."

"I've seen elephants," protested Jamie. "I've been to the zoo and the circus plenty of times."

McClellan laughed, clasping Jamie to him. "He is too young to have been fighting battles. But never fear, I will keep him close to me. I will make him one of my personal orderlies." The General blew his nose on a handkerchief. "I just lost one of my best couriers. Shot down by a Reb sharpshooter. Just a poor little lad of fifteen."

He clapped Jamie on the back. "Go to the Quartermaster's, James. See if they have a nicer uniform for you. Now let me talk alone with Major Allen and my officers. We must plan our immediate pursuit of the foxy Lee while his forces are divided."

"Hold your horses, General!" exclaimed Pinkerton. "Lee's lost dispatch mentions eight different command units. If each unit has, let's say, 15,000 men, that's . . . um . . . over 100,000 men in total, thousands more than we have. One must be cautious, General."

"Hey, Pinky, you can multiply! Good for you!" There was just something about that Pinkerton—so serious, so intense—Jamie couldn't resist teasing him. A bit like Rob!

But important issues were at stake here. Jamie had to help convince McClellan to move quickly.

"Come on, General," urged Jamie. "When did the Rebs ever outnumber us? You have to strike now while their troops are divided. Break through South

Mountain and head them off at the pass! You can still save Harper's Ferry!"

Pinkerton gave him a furious look. "Who do you think you are, you no-account hornswoggler! You don't know beans about warfare!"

Holding up his hand majestically, McClellan silenced both of them as he pulled out a map of the region.

"I must study my terrain," said the General. "We will talk again later."

"Yeah, well, don't wait too long, or you'll lose the upper hand, General," cautioned Jamie, but when Pinkerton moved towards him with murder in his eye, he decided it was time to split. So he saluted farewell and worked his way through the various military officers and businessmen. As Jamie exited, he bumped into someone else leaving, a small man not in uniform, sporting a very full set of whiskers and a hat with a brim wide enough to hide half his face.

"'Scuse me, dude," said Jamie.

The man cleared his throat, then pushed him aside.

Jamie walked down the path behind him, trying to understand his sudden feeling of unease. Something about that throat clearing sounded familiar, and he watched the man's gait as he walked briskly away.

"R . . . Rob?"

****

Chapter 10

The Surrender of Harper's Ferry

HARPER'S FERRY, WEST VIRGINIA: MONDAY, SEPTEMBER 15, 1862

In the early morning mist, Rob jostled along in the food-laden wagon. Still wearing civilian clothes but without the fake whiskers, he fingered his wide-brimmed hat and tried to decide if it was a pang of guilt that he felt. Had it been right to squeal on General McClellan like that? He had never liked the man, historically speaking, that is, and had often wondered why President Lincoln, so wise and clever in so many other ways, had had such faulty judgement when it came to picking his generals. General McClellan was vain, emotional, and cautious to the point of ineptitude, in no way a match for the bold General Lee. Besides, if Rob hadn't told that Reb soldier, who told the Confederate head of cavalry "Jeb" Stuart, who told General Lee, about finding the lost dispatch, one of those pro-Southern Frederick businessmen would have. For that was historically what had happened. Knowing McClellan would be swift on their trail—well, knowing Mac, maybe not so swift—to Harper's Ferry, Lee had ordered troops to block the passes through South Mountain, leading to the famous

Battle of South Mountain. Rob didn't believe he could really change the course of history . . . or could he?

"Got any family?" asked the farmer driving the wagon, trying to make conversation. Rob had hitched a ride in the direction of Harper's Ferry from a farmer going to market. He had wanted to get away from the Battle of South Mountain. When he had read about it, it had always given him the creeps, occurring as it did on slippery high mountain ridges, fighting Indian style among the rocks and trees, with the Rebels finally in such hasty retreat that they had just left their dead and wounded on the mountain where they had fallen. Instead, Rob hoped to witness the more glorious Confederate victory he knew was in store at Harper's Ferry.

"Why, sure, parents and all."

"Any brothers or sisters?"

"Just a younger brother," replied Rob, and that pang of guilt throbbed. Maybe it wasn't McClellan he felt guilty about, maybe it was ignoring Jamie like that, pretending not to know him. Well, it would have blown his disguise! Still . . .

"Guard him well, and stand up for each other," said the farmer. "Friends is friends, but brothers is forever."

"Yeah, right, blood is thicker than water, and all that," retorted Rob cynically.

"Well, young 'un," he said, biting into one of the ripe red apples he was bringing to market, "you may think I'm just spouting, but take it from me, the bond between brothers is the strongest in the world. I've lost my horse, and my wife run off, but it's havin' my brother killed at the Battle of Bull Run that hurt me the most." He gave Rob a sharp look along with an apple. "War is a terrible thing, boy. Don't ever make the mistake of glorifying it."

"Well, I just want to get to Harper's Ferry, all right? I'm not expecting a big battle there."

The farmer wagged a finger at him. "Oh, but I seen all the cannon them Rebs dragged up those mountains. An' I heard the two sides blastin' away at each other yesterday. Them Rebs comin' from all sides aim to surround 'em, I'd wager. I reckon I'm plum crazy to go there. But a man's got to earn his daily bread."

"Really that bad, huh?" said Rob, acting as if he didn't care, though his heart skipped a beat from nervousness. How he hated the sound of cannon!

"An' where oh where is General McClellan to save the day? Just tell me that, hmm?"

"You better not count on that puffed-up piece of—"

Rob stopped himself, but not in time. The farmer turned to squint at him through the heavy fog. "Are you a Reb sympathizer, young 'un?"

Before he could answer, the sound of cannon firing from three different directions blasted through the air. In the distance, they saw bright bursts of orange and yellow followed by a ring of heavy smoke.

"Whoa, horsy! The battle's begun!" cried the farmer. Together they crouched down behind the wagon, listening to the intense bombardment. Rob cringed. This was the loudest cannon fire he had ever heard or even imagined before.

"Jest whistle a tune, boy. It always helps me."

Together they whistled "Oh, Suzanna," "Way Down Upon the Swannee River," "Rock of Ages," "Amazing Grace," "Auld Lang Syne," and, finally, after the hour-long bombardment ended and they could see far in the distance a Union man on horseback waving a white flag of surrender, "Dixie."

Cautiously, they began to get back into the wagon when a sudden burst of artillery from the Confederates froze them in their tracks. A blood-curdling scream split the air as someone fell.

"That's Colonel Miles," Rob thought, shivering to himself, "commander of the whole Union garrison. Both his legs shot off. A slow and painful death. And among his last words were, 'where is McClellan and his army?'"

"Hardly sportin'," complained the farmer, "after the Feds raised the white flag an' all."

"Probably just couldn't see it in all the fog and smoke," said Rob. "It's not like the Rebs to cheat like that."

Then, once again, silence.

Slowly, somberly, they trotted into Harper's Ferry.

****

The morning fog lifted and the town looked pretty as a postcard, nestled in the mountains between two broad rivers. But what really caught Rob's eye was the sight of 11,000 Federal soldiers lining the main street, all prisoners of war, side by side with the Rebs. The prisoners didn't seem particularly worse for wear, and many of them craned their necks as if looking for someone. It didn't take Rob long to figure out who it was.

Slowly, with dignity, on his mangy old horse in his soiled gray uniform and filthy forage cap, General Stonewall Jackson rode down the street. Rob took off his cap to show respect. And then, much to his amazement, his gesture spread and soon thousands of Federal soldiers were doffing their caps and cheering their old foe.

A Federal soldier next to him muttered under his breath, "Well, he's not much for looks, boys, but if we'd had him on our side we wouldn't have been caught in this trap!"

****

One hour later, still dressed in civilian clothes, Rob hung back, watching as half-starving Rebel soldiers scooped their fists into the sutler's big wooden barrels of rock candy. They stuffed the candy into their mouths, filling up their pockets too. They were acting like children at Christmas time, thought Rob, hardly like the toughened men of war they had seemed such a short time ago.

A gray-haired sutler rushed out from behind his counter in alarm. "What in blazes are you men doing? Don't you believe in paying for your goods?"

Several soldiers threw some tattered yellowed bills on the counter. "Here ya are, ya greedy li'l man!"

The sutler peered through his spectacles at the strange-looking currency. "Bank of Chattanooga?" He flipped a bill over and saw it was printed on only one side. "What kind of worthless dollars are these?"

"That's good ol' Confederate shucks, Mister," said a soldier, displaying rows of rotten teeth as he popped some more candy in his mouth. He pointed his musket at the sutler's head. "You got a problem with that?"

The sutler shook his head, then offered Rob a tin of food. "Ever try canned lobster, boy?"

"Hey, gimme that!" said another, snatching it away as he filled his haversack to the brim with cans of meat and fistfuls of crackers.

"Looky here! Real honest-to-goodness coffee!" cheered another, dragging sacks of coffee beans down from the shelves. "Goodbye, Jeff Davis coffee!"

Rob knew the men were hungry, even starving, but their greed was beginning to bother him. He walked outside and was almost run over by a horse. "Here, horsy, horsy! Come to your new master!" A Reb soldier lassoed a rope around the horse's neck and dragged the animal to him. He loaded the horse up with bags of confiscated goodies.

Rob walked into the quartermaster depot where he found Confederates going through piles of Federal uniforms. Eager Rebs were tearing off their tattered gray jackets and putting on spanking new blue ones. "Jest in time for the winter!" crowed one.

"But you'll look like a damned Yankee," said his friend.

"What of it? At least I'll be warm at night! Hey, look over here—blankets! Next best thing to havin' my sweetheart near me!"

"Shoes!" cried a barefoot Rebel.

One soldier tried on a blue shell jacket so tight he could only get one arm in. "Dang it, only a midget could wear this one." He caught sight of Rob and threw it at him. "Here, boy, you're a small one. You'll be needin' a jacket 'fore too long. Maryland nights gets mighty cold, ah hear tell."

Before Rob could object, the soldier was draping it over his shoulders. "Hey, ain't that a purty fit!" A sudden look of suspicion crossed his face. Ya are a southern boy, ain't ya? Ya ain't one of those Yank boys tryin' to sneak out of town, are ya?"

"Oh, yes, ah'm a Confederate." Rob nodded his head vigorously. "Ah shore am."

The soldier clapped him on the back. "Well, have some fun here at Harper's Ferry an' enjoy it while ya can, boy. Ol' Stonewall said to cook two days' rations 'fore we leave, so I reckon there's some hard marchin' ahead!"

Just then, Rob heard the sound of angry voices and he caught sight of Stonewall Jackson, quarreling with an equally scruffy-looking officer. Rob was surprised because Stonewall Jackson was just not the kind of man with whom most people would dare argue. Intrigued, Rob moved closer to steal a better look at the other man. The officer looked slightly younger than

Jackson, in his late 30's, with a thin face featuring high cheekbones, a reddish beard, and long dirty hair. His thigh-high black boots were covered with mud, as were his yellow gauntlets, gloves which went almost to his elbows. From his belt dangled a saber on one side, a revolver on the other.

"Now see here, just because I let you lead your men here at the siege of Harper's Ferry doesn't mean you're not still under arrest," snapped Jackson.

The younger man's eyes spit fire. "Let me hear the charges then. Would you dare accuse me of failure to march my men according to schedule? You, whose troops are always late, who have placed my Light Brigade in mortal danger at two, no make it three, previous battles."

"You were insubordinate, Hill. And you are in danger of repeatin' that mistake at this very moment."

Wow, thought Rob. That's A. P. Hill, one of the bravest fighters in the whole Confederate army. It seemed too bad he and that other heroic figure, Stonewall Jackson, couldn't get along.

"You gave my men marching orders when I was standing right there, General Jackson . . . violating the chain of command and humiliating me in front of my men."

Jackson held up his hand. "There is plenty of time for us to finish this quarrel after the campaign. Let us put our differences aside for now. I am putting you personally in charge of the surrender of the garrison here."

Hill looked slightly mollified.

"Now I want you to be generous to a fault, General Hill. Once you check all these prisoners through, I want you to free them as long as they sign the oath."

"Oath?" asked Hill, concentrating fiercely on the task at hand.

"You know, the usual thing. Swearing they won't take up arms against the Confederacy until an exchange of prisoners can be arranged. Supply them with two days of rations. Oh, and let the officers keep their sidearms, and any other personal baggage they may have," he added.

Hill looked at him incredulously.

"And lend them wagons to transport their things."

Hill's mouth dropped open. "You want to lend Yankees our own wagons to move their personal belongings? How can we trust the Yankees to return anything?"

"War may be a fiendish business," said Jackson. "But we should always behave like the true gentlemen of Virginia we are. And then the enemy will do likewise. Besides. . . ," he added, grinning, picking up a spanking new Springfield rifle that was still packed in its crate. He sighted along it, then put it down reluctantly. ". . . I figure we have just gained over 10,000 muskets, seventy or eighty cannon, and about 200 wagons. We can afford to be generous."

Then Jackson got up on his horse. "I must send word to General Lee of our great victory. God has been kind."

"How's your back, General?" Rob could not resist asking.

Jackson looked startled, but then recognized him. "Henry, is it not? Have you got separated from your unit again, boy?"

Rob nodded, then saluted. The man's memory was phenomenal.

"Henry, fall in there with A. P. Hill's division." He tossed Rob one of the rifles stacked in the crate. "He's going to need some more good men."

Off the General rode in a whirl of dust.

Hill studied Rob, who was pretending to take aim with the rifle. "Know your firearms, soldier? Sure beats our old smoothbore! Well, come along then. Old Stonewall's right—we could use some more men."

****

Chapter 11

"Strong an' Capable Hands"

FREDERICK, MARYLAND: SUNDAY, SEPTEMBER 14, 1862

Sarah watched some Federal troops as they passed by Alexander's photographic buggy. When the Union troops had first marched into Frederick, they had received a much warmer welcome than the Rebels had. Townspeople had cheered them. Small children had run from their houses to offer water; and women had handed out homebaked pies and cakes, especially to the more handsome soldiers.

"I wonder where Rob and Jamie are," Sarah wondered aloud.

"Finding those boys could take awhile, lass. So many soldiers around, it would be like finding two needles in a haystack. An' if you stick with me, you'd best be remembering I have work to do. I have photographic pictures to take, and this time I aim to place me own name on them."

Sarah scrutinized the man seated next to her driving their wagon. "Is that why you wanted to time travel, Alexander? To show it was you and not Mathew Brady who took all those photographs?"

"Partly that. I do hate to see someone take the credit for something he never did." He gently prodded his horse forward. "But I had other motives too, lass. I wanted to learn more about modern photography, to improve my technique and such. Y'see, if I can make truly powerful pictures of the dead an' wounded, and folks see the true horror of it all, maybe men will stop marching off to war."

"I'm sorry to be the one to tell you this," said Sarah. "But there'll be more wars after the Civil War. I don't suppose you know about World War I and World War II. Not to mention Korea and Vietnam."

Alexander looked at her sadly and Sarah sighed, depressed. "I'm tired and hungry."

"There's an inn up ahead. We'll stop and partake of some nourishment. But I warn you, child, I must keep up with the army if I'm to take my battle pictures."

Sarah looked down at her smooth white hands, the pink polish on her nails now chipped away. "Actually, it's nice meeting an idealist, someone who cares about people. I've never really had a chance to do anything for anyone."

Alexander halted his horse in front of the inn. "Everyone has some good in 'em, lass. 'Tis only a matter of bein' in the right place at the right time to bring it out."

As he helped Sarah down from the seat, he picked up one of her hands. "Oh, I'm certain these pretty hands could be capable of doing great works if they had only the opportunity."

As Alexander tied up his horse at the inn's hitching post, a large covered wagon pulled by six mules lurched to a stop in a cloud of dust. The wagon was piled so high with boxes overflowing with bandages, dressings, lanterns, pickled and canned foods, that it almost tipped over.

"By God," said Alexander. "I dinna ever see mules move quite so fast."

A tiny middle-aged woman wearing a plain, dark print skirt and blouse and a huge bonnet jumped down from the wagon seat. She turned to a sweet-faced young man still sitting in the wagon, telling him, "I'll only be a minute, Cornie. Just seeing if the inn has any bread for sale. Don't try to help me, you'll only slow us down!"

The man nodded obediently. "Yes, Miss Barton."

Alexander stared at this dynamo of a woman, until his manners reminded him to remove his cap. "Miss Clara Barton, I presume?"

She tapped her boot impatiently. "Yes. Do I know you?"

Alexander bowed. "Alexander Gardner, in the employ of Mathew Brady, photographic gallery. I have been so longing to take your portrait, Madam. If you have the time . . . "

"Sorry, no time." Then, as if realizing her rudeness, she gave him a coquettish smile and offered her hand. "Do come see me after the war, my dear man. But please write me at least a fortnight before the date." She patted her hair anxiously. "My hair can look such a fright some days."

"Your hair is not important, dear lady. 'Tis the strength of character writ upon your face that interests me." He looked down at her hands. "Aye, you've strong an' capable hands like a man's."

"Hmph," she snorted, as if unsure whether it was meant as a compliment. "Excuse me, sir, I have bread to purchase. Battle could break out at any time and I have to be able to feed my wounded men." And she swooped past them into the inn, her long skirts sweeping the floor in front of them.

Sarah blinked in surprise. "That's *the* Clara Barton?"

"Aye, lass. Have you heard of her even in your times?"

"You bet! I wrote a whole paper on her for my American History course. She was really ahead of her time for women. And so dedicated to helping the sick and wounded. Would I ever love to talk to her!"

"Well, you will have little chance of that, lass. I dinna think that she will stop for a chat just now."

As they walked into the inn, they heard Miss Barton's sharp voice. "What do you mean, you have no more than one or two loaves of bread to sell? An inn in a town the size of Frederick?" Suddenly, she burst into tears, wringing her hands. "Oh, my dear man, I wanted this bread for the sick and wounded! Whatever shall I do now?"

"There, there, Madam," said the innkeeper, clearly upset by her tears. "Let me see what's in the kitchen." He scurried from the room.

"Thank you, thank you," she called out, pressing her handkerchief to her face.

"Ms. Barton?" Sarah tapped her on the shoulder.

Miss Barton whirled around, dry eyed and all business now.

"Why do you say 'Miz'? Are you from the South, young lady?"

"Oh, no, Miss Barton. I'm Sarah Singleton from Rockville, Maryland."

"Rockville. A good town." She raised her voice so she could be heard by the staff. "*They* provided me with plenty of good bread."

"Miss Barton, do you think I could travel with you for awhile?"

"I'm on my way to a battleground, not a Sunday picnic."

"Well, I could help you get there. People always tell me I have a good sense of direction."

Miss Barton looked at her skeptically.

"And I'll help you tend the wounded. I've had medical training, you know." She wondered if a Girl Scout First Aid badge was stretching the truth a bit.

Miss Barton looked at her again, this time with penetrating dark eyes she felt could see into her very soul. "Do you faint at the sight of blood? Because if you do, don't waste my time. I'm fed up to here with ladies such as that."

Sarah reflected for a minute before answering. "No, blood doesn't bother me so much."

"I used to like having some ladies with me—better for my reputation, I thought." Miss Barton stuck out her chin defiantly. "But you know, I just don't care what people may say anymore. Cornelius Welles is faithful to my orders and calm under fire, and enough help for me, thank you very much. I know he won't run away at the first sound of cannon fire."

"I won't either, Miss Barton. I've heard cannon fire before and it doesn't scare me a bit." I'm not even lying, she thought to herself, thinking of the battle reenactments she had attended.

"You'll have to sleep on the hard floor of the wagon with me. Cornie and my driver sleep on the ground outside. When we have any time for sleep, that is."

"That doesn't bother me. I need very little sleep."

"Hmph. You are stubborn."

"Excuse me for saying so, but so are you."

At that, Miss Barton burst into laughter and for a moment she looked almost girl-like, instead of a middle-aged woman with the cares of the world on her shoulders. Suddenly, her nostrils quivered at the aroma of freshly baked bread. Back from the kitchen bustled the innkeeper and his staff, bearing tray after tray of fragrant white bread fresh from the oven.

Miss Barton looked triumphant. "So you did have more bread, after all! All right, young lady, I haven't the time nor the patience to argue with you. Come along, if you must, and we'll test your mettle. I'm sure I can use an extra pair of hands."

Smiling broadly, Sarah turned to the shocked Alexander, holding out her hand to him. "Bye, Mr. Gardner. Now we'll find out if these hands are good for anything. If you see either of my friends, tell them I'm with Clara Barton, won't you?"

Alexander removed his cap and shook her hand vigorously. "Good-bye, Sarah. I must say, you have grit. I can see why the Henry boys are so smitten with you." He suddenly thought of something. "Wait a minute, lass, you said you were tired and hungry and I promised to get you some refreshment here!"

Miss Barton was busily loading dozens and dozens of bread loaves into her already stuffed wagon. Sarah rushed over to help her. "Well, there's plenty of bread here!" called Sarah gaily and she waved good-bye as the carriage lurched into the distance.

****

MONDAY, SEPTEMBER 15, 1862

On the road, men in soiled blue uniforms began trudging towards them. "Anything to eat, ladies?" said one exhausted young soldier.

"Sarah, give the boy some bread," barked Miss Barton. Sarah cut off a generous slice from one of their newly acquired loaves.

"Not so much," said Miss Barton. "These loaves will mean life or death to the wounded men."

The soldier devoured the piece of bread. "God bless you, ladies."

Soon a dozen soldiers surrounded them. Sarah cut up several loaves and distributed the bread as fast as she could, knowing she would be scolded if she slowed Miss Barton's wagon down for more than a few minutes.

Ahead loomed the heavily wooded ridge of South Mountain. "Full chisel, driver!" shouted Clara Barton.

"Where are you ladies going in such a rush?" cried one of the soldiers. "We just had a terrible battle there yesterday! Why, the blood hasn't even cooled yet!"

"It ain't no place for ladies," said another soldier, addressing his remarks to Cornelius and the driver. "Better head back toward Middletown, or all the way back to Frederick."

"Balderdash!" exclaimed Barton. "I've a whole wagon full of medical supplies. If a battlefield's not the place for me, where is, boys?" And she snatched the whip from the driver and whipped the mules herself.

They trotted up the mountain until they reached the open swale known as Turner's Gap.

"Whoa!" One of the mules had almost tripped over a dead horse. Slowly, the mules picked their way through many other carcasses, in addition to broken wheels, abandoned muskets, haversacks, and canteens. Cannonballs were strewn across the field. But far worse sights were in store. Soon they saw men, or what had once been men, their bodies stiff and blackened in the noonday sun, the stench of decaying flesh heavy in the air.

Sarah felt like she was going to be sick, but she tried to hide it. Shooting a quick glance at Miss Barton, she saw that the hardened lady herself looked the way Sarah felt.

"Are you all right, Miss Barton?" she asked, worried.

"The truth is, Sarah, that this is the first time I've ever been on a battlefield." She took a deep breath. "Let's look for the wounded."

A group of gravediggers heard her words. "There ain't no wounded here, ma'am. Only thing to do now is to bury the dead."

Sarah looked at the scene in horror. Row upon row, there lay the dead. They may have been Blues; they may have been Grays. Whichever they were no longer mattered. For they all looked the same color now—black—bloated and dead in the afternoon sun.

****

Chapter 12

Picnic at Pry's

SHARPSBURG, MARYLAND: MONDAY, SEPTEMBER 15, 1862

"A glorious victory!" exulted General McClellan. Jamie saw the General was in high spirits today. "We whipped those Rebels good at South Mountain, did we not, George my boy?"

"Yes, sir," said Captain George Armstrong Custer. His long yellow curls bobbed in agreement. "Are you sure about that Pry house, sir?"

"Of course I am! That house has the best view of the land for miles! It will give me a bird's-eye view of the coming battle."

"But what if Mr. Pry refuses?"

McClellan struck a Napoleonic pose, right hand thrust inside the left breast of his well-tailored frock coat. "Surely he will feel honored by our request." He suddenly took notice of Jamie standing near him. "Take the boy with you. He can act as your courier."

Jamie awkwardly galloped with about a dozen officers along Boonsboro Turnpike. They turned off at a tree-lined dirt lane which led toward a handsome red brick farmhouse perched high on a steep hill. A middle-aged

78

farmer, flanked by his wife and four young sons, stepped out of the house at the sound of their horses.

Captain Custer leaped off his horse with his usual dramatic dash.

"Mr. Philip Pry?"

The farmer eyed him suspiciously. "Yes . . . what can I do for you?"

"Mr. Pry, a great honor is to be bestowed upon you!"

"Hmm?"

"General McClellan wishes to make his headquarters at your home."

"You mean, jest put him up and feed him for a few days?"

"Well, just him and his closest officers."

Mrs. Pry looked nervous. "How many would that be?"

"Oh, just a few dozen or so."

Mr. and Mrs. Pry looked aghast.

"Oh, and there'll probably be a few troop regiments, too," Custer added. "Part of the Second Corps will bivouac here."

"Do we have to feed all of them?" asked Mrs. Pry.

"Oh, don't worry about feeding the soldiers." The captain looked around at the lush rows of apple trees, the fruit just red enough for picking, and the fields filled with stalk after stalk of fully ripened corn. "They'll just sort of . . . help themselves."

Mrs. Pry threw her apron over her face and wailed.

"Yes, sir," concluded Captain Custer. "It's a real honor for you folks." He leaped back onto his horse and started to go. "Oh, by the way . . . the General loves . . . um . . . Southern fried chicken."

****

Soon, the house on the hill became a beehive of activity. Hundreds of tents for the troops were erected in the farmer's fields. Telescopes were driven by stake into the Pry's front yard, with armchairs from the Pry's parlor set up close by for comfortable viewing. Signal flags were hung from tall poles. Supply wagons rattled up and down the dirt road.

Among a group of officers Jamie stood next to the General, who peered down below through one of the telescopes. Also next to the General was Mr. Pry, who nervously watched all the activity around his house.

"I had hoped maybe we had driven the Rebs out of Maryland. But my reports say they have come back for more punishment." McClellan clapped Mr. Pry on the back. "Yes, indeed, Mr. Pry. We will be watching history unfold here, right from your very house, in just a couple of days."

"A couple of days, sir?" asked Jamie. "I know I'm just a lowly courier boy, but don't you think maybe you should strike now? I mean, that 'lost dispatch' showed how Jackson split off from Lee's forces, he's probably still in Harper's Ferry, and—"

McClellan laughed. "Ah, impetuous youth! How little you understand all a general must do! First, I must determine where the enemy is, how many are out there, then map out a battle plan, all the while carefully studying the terrain . . . ." Through the heavy morning mist, he pointed to the broad expanse of green grass and corn fields bordered by Antietam Creek far down below them.

"Ah, now this will be a grand site for a battle! Not a rock, not a crevice for the Rebs to hide in." He leaned close to Mr. Pry. "I hope to give that Bobby Lee the whipping of his life!"

Mr. Pry cleared his throat nervously. "Umm, a big battle you're expecting . . . right below us?"

"Do not worry, Mr. Pry. We will make sure you and your family are transported safely to the rear before the battle begins. You have friends in the neighborhood you can stay with?"

Mr. Pry shrugged.

"Confound it, Jamie boy," fretted the General, peering through his telescope into the mist. "If only I knew where those Rebs were. I know they are out there, maybe not more than a few miles from where we stand. If I only knew where!"

Pinkerton came bustling towards them. "Bad news, General. My latest calculations tell me that Lee's army has grown by at least 15,000 men."

"See what I'm saying, sir?" persisted Jamie. "Why not attack now before Stonewall Jackson arrives from Harper's Ferry with his reinforcements?"

Pinkerton glared at him. "Mr. Military Expert, what unit did you say you were drumming with?"

"Umm . . . 16th Connecticut."

"I'm checking it out, James Henry. Checking it out."

"But you know how those army records are always screwed up, don't ya, Pinky?"

Pinkerton flushed with anger, moving his face close to Jamie's. "Don't you ever . . . ever call me that again. I'm Major Allen."

"Sure you are, dude." Jamie had an idea and decided it was time to change the subject. "Hey, General, sir, what happens when you ride among your men?"

McClellan lifted his head proudly. "Why, my men go wild, of course! They wave their caps and give such rousing cheers they can be heard for miles!"

"Well, sir, if the Rebs heard all that noise, don't you think they might be tempted to take a potshot?"

"A potshot?"

"You know, fire their artillery at you."

McClellan's face lit up with a smile. "Oh, I under-stand your drift now. You mean, they would expose their position when they fire at me?"

Jamie nodded.

McClellan slapped him on the back. "Brilliant idea, boy! Brilliant!"

Jamie beamed. Maybe Rob wasn't the only smart one in the family.

"Sir, that's a horrible idea!" cried one of McClellan's officers. "What if you were to get shot?"

In a tense voice, Pinkerton said, "You must stay here at headquarters, General. To deliberately expose yourself to Rebel batteries would be reckless and ill-advised."

"No pain, no gain," said Jamie, giving the General a wink.

****

The mist cleared. Side by side with General McClellan and the usual cluster of favorite officers, Jamie galloped down the hill to the first group of Union troops. Just as the General had predicted, all hell broke loose as the men recognized their famous leader.

"That's General McClellan, boys!" cried a soldier.

"With him at our side, we know we'll win!" cried another.

"Three cheers for Little Mac!" cried another, lead-ing the men in a rousing cheer.

The three cheers had barely died and the echo was still reverberating in the valley when a sudden volley of artillery almost hurled Jamie from his horse.

"Darn!" Jamie thought to himself. "Me and my bright ideas!"

McClellan turned to one of his officers, pointing to where the hostile salvo had come from. "Make a note of that Rebel position, Captain!"

And off they galloped to visit another unit.

"Here comes McClellan!"

This is getting real old real fast, thought Jamie.

Again the men burst into cheers, caps thrown into the air. "Little Mac! Little Mac! Hurrah!" BOOM went another round of Rebel artillery.

McClellan pointed out another direction. "Aha! More Rebs! Brilliant idea, Jamie boy. At this rate, we will know all their positions by noon time. To celebrate, let us have a picnic dinner at the Pry House, men. My treat!"

Jamie tried to smile and look appreciative. But he was getting sore from all the horseback riding, felt exhausted from dodging artillery, was weary of hanging around with the pompous General and his staff, and was especially sick and tired of breaking his jaws eating hardtack. Oh, for the sight of golden arches! "Yes, sir, Big Mac," he muttered.

****

Chapter 13

Finding the Front

ROAD TO SHARPSBURG:

MONDAY EVENING, SEPTEMBER 15, 1862

A beautiful sunset spread across the sky, but Sarah did not enjoy it. She was too busy coughing from the dust raised by ten miles of army wagons strung out along the road.

Miss Barton looked at Sarah with concern. "You all right, child?"

"I'm fine, Miss Barton. I just had no idea the pollution was so bad in this period."

Miss Barton gave her a quizzical look. "Pollution? This period?"

"I just meant all the dust in the air."

"You do talk queerly, child," Miss Barton snapped. "Oh, I'm sorry, Sarah. It's just I'm as mad as a March hare! Look at all this traffic. Here I have a load full of life-saving supplies, and by the time I get to Sharpsburg, half the men will be dead from lack of proper medical attention."

"I know you'll make it in time," Sarah reassured her.

Miss Barton looked at her sharply. "How would you know? You're not one of those mystic people claiming the gift of foresight, are you?"

"Let's just say I believe in you."

"Hmph." Miss Barton examined a map she spread out on her lap. "There must be some kind of shortcut."

Sarah peered over her shoulder, trying to help. But the roads were so changed from the ones she knew that she could not recognize any landmarks.

All around them, they began noticing men halting their horses and taking supplies out of their saddle bags. Soon, scores of campfires sprang up by the side of the road as hundreds of men began cooking their suppers and getting ready to bed down for the night.

After a simple meal of leathery beef stew cooked over a fire, Sarah and Miss Barton rolled up in their woolen blankets among all the piles of supplies inside the wagon.

"Good night, Miss Barton."

"'Night, Sarah. Sleep well, for we may not get the chance again for quite some time."

For hours, Sarah tossed and turned. The wagon floor felt hard against her back. She could hear Cornelius and the driver snoring on the ground outside. Could she stand the heat of battle, she wondered. Would she be able to help Miss Barton when men dripping with blood fell at her feet? Could she stand the sight of . . . amputations?

"You awake, Sarah?"

Sarah turned toward Miss Barton. "I sure am."

Miss Barton leaped to her feet. "Well, what are we waiting for? Let's pass all those sleepyheads and get on to Sharpsburg! Cornie!"

Cornelius Welles stumbled to the wagon, wiping the sleep from his eyes.

"But, Ma'am—it's one o'clock in the morning!"

"Cornie, how can you think of sleep when men may be out there dying already?"

"Yes, Ma'am," he said, rolling up his blanket and shaking the driver awake. "Come on, fellow, Miss Barton says it's time to roll!"

And while the other wagons sat parked on the road, their drivers snoring away, Clara Barton and her supply wagon snaked past them and made their way through the dark Maryland countryside toward a once sleepy town named Sharpsburg.

****

TUESDAY, SEPTEMBER 16, 1862

"My boys, my boys!" Clara's eyes filled with tears as she looked on the faces of the men of the 21st Massachusetts. "These are my very own hometown boys."

It was noon. Clara's dusty wagon halted at General Ambrose Burnside's headquarters on a wooded hill overlooking a large stone bridge across the creek. Sarah watched the young men hug and hang on Clara as they would their own mother. Clara gave the men loaves of bread and coffee powder mixed with sugar.

"Hey, I thought that bread was for the wounded men," objected the driver.

"But these are my boys!" She hugged several more, slicing off extra thick slices of bread for them.

Major General Ambrose E. Burnside strode out of his headquarters to see what all the commotion was about. He was a tall, imposing man, a bit on the plump side, with a huge moustache connected to the full fuzzy sideburns for which he was justly famous.

"Women on the battlefield?" he asked, shocked.

"It's Clara Barton, General, and her beautiful assistant!" said a soldier.

"Oh . . . Clara Barton, I should have known! Well, Miss Barton, I've read about your nursing exploits in the newspapers. Got any extra bread for me?"

In his big boots, dark blue uniform, and high-crowned hat, Sarah could hardly take her eyes off the towering figure. Now this man looked like a general! But Clara seemed less impressed.

"Tell me the quickest way to McClellan's head-quarters and I'll be glad to give you a loaf, General Burnside," snapped Miss Barton. It was clear she had little use for this affable but ponderous man.

"Always have to be in the heart of the action, don't you, Miss Barton? Well, now, I'm a little annoyed at General McClellan right now, and if you see him, I don't mind if you tell him so, straight from his old school chum. First, he separates me from my own men at South Mountain, then he orders me to take over Major General Reno's troops who are leaderless since he fell dead over there."

"So what's wrong with that?" muttered Clara.

Burnside looked at her as if she was crazy. "Don't you understand, my dear woman? Jake Cox is their ranking division commander and so he should be the one to take over the Ninth Corps, not me."

Clara waggled some bread temptingly near him. "I have little interest in your power squabbles. Just tell me how to get to McClellan's headquarters."

Burnside smacked his lips. "All right, all right. Just stay on the east bank of Antietam Creek and go north a few miles. He's at the big red brick house up on the hill. The Pry house. Can't miss it."

Clara gave him the bread and Burnside doffed his cap politely. "They probably have good food over there," he sighed. "Can you bring me back a leg of chicken or two?"

Impatiently she turned her back on him. "Come, Sarah, Cornie. Let's find General McClellan and find out what's really going on."

They sprang back into their wagon and drove off in a cloud of dust, the soldiers still waving and blowing kisses to Miss Clara Barton and her beautiful assistant.

****

PRE-DAWN, WEDNESDAY MORNING, SEPTEMBER 17, 1862

The women camped out in their wagon on the Pry house hillside. Unable to sleep, they lay listening to the patter of the rain punctuated by the occasional picket cross fire. They were not alone. Thousands of men were also unable to sleep that night, as they lay tensed and ready for the coming battle.

Clara Barton started coughing. Sarah bolted upright.

"Are you all right, Miss Barton?"

"I've been fighting off a fever ever since I left Washington. I just hope to God it isn't typhoid."

Sarah shuddered at the words. Was typhoid fever contagious? Oh, well, she told herself, that was the least of her worries. She tucked another blanket around Clara.

"Thank you, dear. You've really been a Godsend."

Sarah warmed to the rare words of praise.

Suddenly, they heard the distant sound of gunfire.

"Oh, my God, could it be starting already? It's not even daybreak. Come with me, Sarah."

Clara grabbed a pair of field glasses and together they climbed farther up the hill. Even at the top, they could see nothing in the dark and mist. The gunfire had stopped as suddenly as it had started. The two women shuddered in the early morning chill, as they listened to the stirrings of McClellan and his staff.

First light of dawn. A cannon roared, soon joined by another and another until Sarah's ears buzzed and the sky filled with smoke.

Suddenly, a cheer arose from the tree tops around her. "Hurray for Fightin' Joe!" yelled men who had climbed trees to get a better view of the battlefield.

Clara raised her binoculars to see what the men were cheering. "It's Hooker's First Corps! They're charging over in the corn field!" cried Clara, grabbing Sarah by the hand. "Come, I think I know where the battle is! Cornie!"

They raced back to their wagon, pausing only long enough for Cornelius and the driver to climb quickly in. Clara studied her map. "Boonsboro Turnpike! At full speed!"

"Wait a minute!" Sarah snatched the map away for a moment. "I think I see a shortcut."

Following Sarah's directions, with the roar of cannon and musket fire spurring them on, the mule-driven buggy careened down a back road off Boonsboro Turnpike leading across an old bridge across Antietam Creek. They turned down Smoketown Road. There, they saw a white-haired old gentleman in high-ranking uniform, bleeding profusely, carried by five soldiers who had formed a chair for him with their muskets to remove him from the battle front.

Sarah ran to help the old man, but the soldiers shooed her away.

"It's General Mansfield," said one of the soldiers. "We've already called for his surgeon."

"Not that it matters," added another. "He's a goner. You ladies stay to the rear or you'll be in the same condition as our General here."

They dumped Mansfield by a tree, doffed their caps to the ladies, and ran back toward the battle, grim-faced.

Moving northeast of the battleground, the women drove through a corn field until they spied an old barn, partially hidden among the high stalks of corn.

"I hear some kind of whining and grunting," said Sarah, who had always had a soft spot for animals. "Maybe there are barn animals trapped inside!"

Clara signaled the driver to halt, then Sarah made her way to the barn. She cautiously opened the door and then stood rigid, shocked at what she saw inside. Clara bustled past her. There, lying in pools of blood on the barn floor, were about three hundred badly wounded men, groaning and writhing in pain.

****

Chapter 14

"Move Your Backside, Burnside!"

LATE WEDNESDAY MORNING, SEPTEMBER 17, 1862

"Come with me, boy," said General McClellan, "I will show you my secret viewing place."

Jamie followed the General up the staircase, glancing into the Pry boys' now empty bedrooms. That morning, at McClellan's insistence, the entire Pry family had been evacuated to the nearby town of Keedysville.

In the hallway, McClellan gestured toward a ladder. Jamie groped his way up the ladder into a dark and musty attic. There, the General jumped onto a trunk and strained to reach a trap door on the ceiling. No doubt about it, there was was a reason they called him "Little Mac." Jamie reached it easily, pushing open the trap door and sticking his head out above the roof. He started to climb onto the roof, but McClellan stopped him.

"Do not be foolhardy. Rebel sharpshooters could drop you like they did my last courier boy. Just put your head out."

From that position, Jamie could see all the way down to the battlefield, though woods and smoke blocked much of the current fighting.

McClellan brushed him aside and trained his binoculars on the view. "Damnation. Those woods are in my way. Let's see what my signal men are showing."

McClellan almost fell off the ladder in his excitement. "Yes! Finally! We took that high ground at the little church! I'll be damned, though, if it didn't take about fifteen times back and forth through that corn field!"

Jamie looked at him questioningly.

"You know, that little whitewashed church near the edge of the woods."

"I know," said Jamie, "but I mean, why was it so important to take the church?"

McClellan looked at him as if he had lost his mind. "Because Johnny Reb was there, boy!"

They clambered back down the ladder, then down the main staircase, to a scene of mad activity. Two men were carrying Major General Joseph Hooker in on a stretcher, his handsome face twisted in pain.

"My God!" cried McClellan. "What has happened to General Hooker? Who's commanding our right flank?"

Hooker took a mouthful of brandy and lifted his bleeding foot. "Got shot in the foot, sir. They're taking me over to the field hospital. I guess that pretty much cuts me out of the action. I ordered George Meade to take over the First Corps."

" 'Fightin' Joe . . . ," murmured Jamie under his breath. "Where's the fight in you now?"

Pinkerton suddenly appeared at his elbow. "I don't see you rushing into battle," he hissed. "And I might add I have heard nothing to confirm your claim that you mustered in with the 16th Connecticut."

"Oh, you know what they say, Pinky. No news is good news."

Pinkerton moved closer to him, flushing with anger. "I warned you never to call me that—"

"You should look at yourself in the mirror. Your face really does turn pink when you get mad."

McClellan stood between them. "Never mind," he said. "This lad has been very useful to me. In fact, I was just planning to assign him some courier duty."

Pinkerton looked at Jamie with open hostility. "Well, we have been losing a lot of couriers lately."

McClellan turned to Pinkerton, exasperated. "I have already sent three couriers to Burn, telling him the same damn thing. He was supposed to cross the creek at the same time that Hooker was pushing toward the church—a coordinated attack, don't you see?"

McClellan drew Jamie close to him. "Now listen, James my boy, we have got to light a fire under Major General Burnside. Tell him General McClellan commands him to push across that bridge and move rapidly up the heights toward Sharpsburg . . . immediately."

A courier came dashing into the house, breathless. "French's division has marched onto the central field, sir. They're moving toward Confederate troops that are positioned in a sunken lane, sir."

McClellan rushed out of the house, Jamie right behind him, to peer through one of the telescopes set up on the front lawn. "Splendid view! James, my boy, come feast your eyes on this grand martial spectacle!"

Jamie looked through the scope to see a perfectly formed brigade, fresh in their bright blue uniforms, bayonets glinting in the late morning sun. They marched up a ridge, keeping rhythm to the jaunty music of their regimental fifes and drums. They had to break formation to scramble across a fence, but immediately went back into their formation as they moved closer and closer to the sunken lane. Jamie watched, fascinated.

Suddenly, a volley of musket fire burst forth from the lane in which the Rebels hid. Jamie watched in horror as he saw many of those beautifully-clad Union soldiers lifted clean off the ground, then slammed down again, blown to bloody bits. Those who survived ran off in panic, only to be turned back by the next brigade marching in from behind them.

Jamie turned away, sick to his stomach. If Rob had thought the Civil War was all glory and heroics, he should take a look at this, he thought.

****

With the sound of the fierce musket fire coming over from Bloody Lane pounding in his ears, Jamie galloped down the hill and followed the creek to Burnside's headquarters.

"Urgent message for General Burnside from General McClellan, sir!" said Jamie, saluting smartly.

An aide motioned him to wait. Jamie watched in horror as group after group of Union soldiers tried to dash across the huge stone bridge, only to be mowed down by Rebel sharpshooters hidden high in trees and behind rocks on the opposite bank.

The aide returned and directed Jamie to where General Burnside sat astride his horse, calmly surveying the same scene of carnage as Jamie. Man, these generals are cold-blooded, thought Jamie, as he rode up to Burnside.

The General glared down at him. "Little Mac has something to say to me, does he? I'll bet he isn't standing over Hooker's shoulder, telling him what to do."

"Relax, General. Fighting Joe is out of commission—he stubbed his little toe on a minie ball."

Burnside's plump, open face could not hide his joy at the news of the setback of his rival. "Well, isn't that a pity."

Jamie continued to stare at the men being fired on as they tried to cross the bridge. "Hey, General, how about having your men wade across the creek upstream where there aren't so many sharpshooters? I mean, what's this obsession with crossing at the bridge?"

Burnside looked puzzled. "Well, I . . . I want my men to have dry feet when they fight. Besides, it's probably too deep to wade across."

"Did you ever check it out, man?"

"This very morning I sent some scouts to investigate that matter. No report from them yet. Rodman's division is to the south of us here. Perhaps they'll be able to wade across. Now tell me your message, boy."

Jamie decided it was no time to mince words. "He said get across the creek! In other words, move your backside, Burnside!"

****

Chapter 15

The Forced March

HARPER'S FERRY: WEDNESDAY AT DAWN, SEPTEMBER 17, 1862

Rob sweated in a hot stuffy upstairs room, as he waited for his turn to speak to A. P. Hill. He was next in line. Rob had bragged to Jamie and Sarah about wanting to fight at Sharpsburg, but now that it looked like he would actually get the chance, he was beginning to get cold feet. If he could just explain to General Hill that this was all some kind of weird time traveling mistake, that he wasn't a Confederate soldier at all, just a teenage reenactor!

Hill drummed his fingers impatiently as he glanced at the documents piled on his desk, and at the long line of men waiting to speak to him. Clearly, Hill was not a "desk job" sort of guy.

"No wonder Jackson made me in charge of the surrender," muttered Hill. "He knew it would make me crazy as a loon. Next!"

A man in the uniform of a Federal cavalry officer stepped up to the desk. "I'm a noncombatant, sir," said the man. "Could you give me a pass to leave Harper's Ferry and go back home to Loudoun County?"

Hill looked him over suspiciously.

"Why are you wearing that uniform if you're not a Yank soldier?"

The man rocked back and forth on his feet. "Umm . . . I bought these clothes from an enlisted man."

Hill leaped to his feet and grabbed the man by the collar. "Liar, don't waste my valuable time! You're as much a civilian as I am. You are henceforth a prisoner of war. And no parole for you, either! Now get out of my sight before I kill you!" He pushed the man out of the room and gave him a kick down the stairs before returning to his desk. "Cowards, I hate 'em all," he muttered, then looked up. "Next?"

Gee, thought Rob, maybe now's not the best time to talk to him.

A courier accompanied by several Confederate officers burst into the room.

"General Hill, an urgent message from General Lee."

Hill's eyes lit up.

"Excuse me, gentlemen," he said and rushed out of the room with the men.

A minute later, Hill returned, his eyes dancing with excitement. He directed one of the officers to his empty seat at the desk. "You take over this job! Any simpleton can do it. Just say 'yes'. . . or 'no.'" Then he left abruptly.

When Hill returned, he was buttoning up a flaming red flannel shirt.

"Oh, oh," muttered a Confederate soldier near Rob. " 'Little Powell' only wears red when he's going into battle."

"Confederate soldiers, come with me!" yelled Hill. "We have an appointment—with destiny!"

Seeing Rob, he grabbed him by the arm. "General Jackson said you're to march with my Light Division. Fall in, son!"

He propelled Rob, along with any other Confederates in the room, out of the building, leaving a line of disgruntled Union soldiers still waiting for their parole.

****

Rob had never known physical punishment as harsh as this.

It had been all right at the beginning. Early in the morning, the men had been fresh and in good spirits. They had full bellies for a change, from all the stores of Yankee food they had taken, and many wore fresh new uniforms stolen from the federal depot. They carried new muskets—Rob did, too—and many of them wore shoes for the first time in months. Not always properly fitting shoes, for they had been confiscated at breakneck speed, but a luxury, nevertheless, for men used to marching barefoot.

But even newly fortified men begin to falter. For A. P. Hill—in his bright red battle shirt, showing beneath his unbuttoned jacket—was like a whirling dervish, waving his sword over his head, riding among his troops, yelling at them to march faster and faster.

Rob knew it was twelve miles as the crow flies from Harper's Ferry to Sharpsburg, but it felt like they had marched farther than that. They must be taking some kind of indirect route in order to avoid the Yanks. Rob's nine-pound rifle felt heavier and heavier, and his arms and shoulders ached more with every step.

Rob was posted near the head of the column, which at first he had thought a disadvantage. But as he glanced to the rear, he saw the men behind him coughing and spitting from all the dust he and the lead troops were raising. Apparently, wearing shoes was a mixed blessing, for shoes raised dust where bare feet had not.

Because he was in good shape from his daily jogging, Rob was able to keep up better than many of the regular soldiers. Marching with Hill meant no rests, no breaks, despite the hot and sticky weather. Man after man collapsed by the side of the road in a state of total exhaustion. Hill did not stop to try to get them up and moving again—he was in too much of a hurry.

"Come on, men! General Lee is depending upon us! Hurry, hurry!"

Rob tried to distract himself from the punishing pace by thinking. First he thought about Sarah. Where was she now? Was she still with Alexander Gardner? Alexander had seemed like a decent sort of guy. And Sarah definitely knew how to take care of herself.

So more and more his worried thoughts turned to his kid brother. Jamie had a way of getting into trouble—his wisecracking, fresh style often amused the girls, but irritated authority figures. If they had drafted him into the Union army, could he make it? Unlike Rob, he had never learned how to shoot a musket. He had no killing instinct in him, none whatsoever. And he was physically soft—he would never survive a grueling march such as this one.

In the distance, a cannon roared, making Rob cringe.

"Give me your sword, coward!" screamed Hill, charging towards him. Rob felt a fresh wave of fear, until he realized he didn't have a sword! Rob looked behind him to see a young officer cowering behind a tree. Trembling, he handed his sword to Hill. THWACK. The sword broke in half on the frightened man's back. He fell into formation—without a sword now—and marched on.

They reached a river. Holding muskets and cartridge boxes high up over their heads, the troops waded across. The water felt cool and refreshing. Rob began gulping down river water and filling his canteen. He knew the water might be dirty, but at this point he hardly cared.

"Stop it!" screamed Hill.

Rob immediately stopped drinking.

"Ehhh . . . shut pan and sing small, or I'll throw you into the drink," snarled a wagon driver, continuing to beat his mule hard. The animal, nearly dying of thirst and fatigue, had stopped midstream and refused to budge. Obviously, the driver did not realize whom he was addressing, for in his red shirt it was not obvious that Hill was the commanding officer. But he found out soon enough. THWACK, went Hill's sword, crashing down hard upon the teamster's back.

Oh, thought Rob to himself, an animal lover. Too bad he doesn't love his men like that. But then Rob imagined the battle ahead. Perhaps this fierce commander was just what the Rebels needed in order to fight—and win.

As Rob marched, he listened to the gunfire growing closer. He was so tired he could barely see straight, much less think. But a sudden chilling thought almost froze him midstep. What if his brother were with the Union troops fighting at Sharpsburg? Would he have to shoot at his own brother?

****

Chapter 16

Jamie Joins His "Friends"

Jamie held his breath, watching. It looked like these particular boys in blue might actually succeed in their mission and cross that stupid bridge! He had watched wave after wave of them charge for the bridge and get slaughtered before they could even reach it.

It would be ironic, Jamie thought, that what had motivated these two regiments of men was not patriotism but whiskey.

Sporting an elegant waxed moustache, Colonel Ferrero was a little man with a big voice, a dancing instructor before the war. He had tried to fire up his men with a rousing appeal to their patriotism. Jamie had almost laughed out loud. As if this little man could inspire these hardened veterans with lofty appeals!

The end of Ferrero's longwinded speech had ended with an appeal: "It is General Burnside's special request that the two 51sts—the 51st of Pennsylvania and the 51st of New York—take that bridge," he boomed. "Will you do it?"

There was a long silence. Finally one of the men snarled cynically, "Will you give us whiskey, Colonel, if we take it?"

"Yep," added another, "you ain't been letting us have our whiskey rations lately."

"Yes, by God," roared Ferrero. "You shall have as much whiskey as you wish! Just take that bridge!"

And with that, the men had squared their shoulders and started down the slope, full speed. Halfway down the hill, the soldiers began dropping from enemy fire, but the ones who made it to the bridge parted, half to the left and half to the right, and ducked for cover under nearby fences and a stone wall that ran along the creek.

The Confederate rifle fire began to slacken. Sensing this, one brave Federal captain dashed onto the bridge. He waved his sword, and a few other men, including the colonel and the flag bearers, followed. Then, before they had a chance to chicken out, men from the two regiments ran onto the bridge from all directions. Halfway across the bridge, the men began to notice a pause in Rebel firing. Out of ammunition? Emboldened, they continued their crazed run.

Only one lone Confederate officer tried to halt them. He ran down to the edge of the creek, waving his sword, and began shouting, "Damned Yankees! You can't cross this bridge! You can't even—"

The men rushing across the bridge pumped him full of bullets and he fell into the stream with a loud splash, his sentence unfinished forever.

"Hurrah!" cried one of the 51st. "We have crossed that cussed bridge!" He looked around him, baffled. "Now what?"

****

Jamie, caught up in their triumph, threw his cap into the air just as the men around him did. "Hurrah!" he yelled. "They did it, they did it! Those crazy dudes crossed the bridge—and all for a lousy shot of whiskey!"

"Yes, it is funny what will motivate a man—even the basest, most cowardly man—to fight," said a familiar voice, close in his ear, and he felt cold metal against his ribs.

Jamie jumped. He turned to see Pinkerton, standing close to him, a pistol in one hand and a musket in the other. A big cigar in his mouth.

"Pinky! Good to see you, man. Did Big Mac send you down here, too? Maybe we can do lunch."

Pinkerton's eyes narrowed. "You . . . are a fraud. A liar and a faker."

Jamie gulped. "What are you talking about, Pinky?"

"I had the muster rolls of the 16th Connecticut checked. There is no record of any James Henry, drummer boy."

Jamie backed away as he talked. "Yeah, well, you know how the bureaucracy is. Always making little boo-boos."

Pinkerton moved in closer. "Acknowledge the corn, boy. I know what you are."

"Hey, do you floss regularly? Or maybe it's all the cigars you smoke, but I really think there's an oral hygiene problem here," chattered Jamie, continuing to back away.

Pinkerton got right in his face. "You might not know what I did before the war . . . ."

"I have a feeling I'm going to find out," said Jamie, looking around him for an escape route. If he started to run, would he get shot in the back?

Pinkerton pointed to his eye.

"What's wrong? Got pink eye?" joked Jamie, desperate now.

" 'The Eye That Never Sleeps,'" intoned Pinkerton. "That was the motto of my detective agency."

"Catchy," said Jamie. "I like it. Maybe you should consider a career in advertising."

Pinkerton jabbed the pistol in his chest. "I watched you when you thought no one was looking. You put those metal things over your ears. You have some kind of newfangled contraption to send out messages to the enemy, don't you, boy?"

"You're hallucinating, dude."

"You . . . are a spy," Pinkerton hissed, spitting out his words along with little flecks of tobacco.

Jamie wiped the spit off his face. "Man, you really do have a problem. Have dentists been invented yet? Umm, look. If I were a spy, would I be hanging around Burn's backside here? I mean, wouldn't I have run over to the Reb side by now to tell him what Big Mac is up to?"

"I don't know," said Pinkerton. "You may be seeking more information before you escape."

"Do I talk like a Reb?"

"You do talk strangely," said Pinkerton. "I've noticed that. That's one reason I became suspicious. That and all the cockamamie ideas you've been giving the General."

"Hey, they've been good ideas! Now, look," said Jamie, trying his most ingratiating smile, "you are not going to be able to prove I'm a spy, and I'm not going to be able to prove I'm not, so what are we going to do about this? You're not going to shoot me down in cold blood, are you? Big Mac's favorite courier?"

Pinkerton smiled back, but it was an evil smile. "You hate fighting, don't you?"

"Well, a little verbal sparring is fine with me. It's the weapons that I'm not so thrilled over—somebody could get hurt, y'know?"

Pinkerton tossed him the musket he'd been carrying.

"You say you were with the 16th Connecticut. Well, there they are! Go out and fight with them, then."

"Well, yeah, they're my boys. But . . . um . . . it's been a long time since I've seen them."

"Liar," hissed Pinkerton. "The unit's only been together for three weeks."

"Yeah, well, I know that, but uh. . . you bond fast during times of war."

"See those men out there moving west into John Otto's corn field?"

Jamie squinted where Pinkerton pointed. "Umm . . . yeah, sure. My good buddies—I recognize them!" He waved. "Hi, Billy! Hi, Norman!"

"Idiot!" hissed Pinkerton. "You couldn't possibly recognize them from here. Now go!" Pinkerton pressed the pistol into his back. "Go and fight with your regiment, you yellow-bellied liar."

"Yes, sir," said Jamie, stumbling down the hill, walking quickly over the bridge, holding his musket awkwardly. "Hey, 16th Connecticut! Wait up, guys! Long time, no see, huh?"

****

Chapter 17

Clash!

"Man, here we are just lying around this corn field, like a bunch of sitting—I mean, lying—ducks," said Jamie.

He was lying on his stomach alongside the other men of the 16th Connecticut, half hidden in the cornstalks. They were isolated from the rest of the troops. Perhaps some order had been given and everyone else had heard it. It was so noisy and smoky from gunfire that that was possible. Jamie only knew that somewhere up there was the enemy. He knew this because he could hear gunfire in the distance.

The teenaged boy next to him, shivering, took a long drink out of a pocket flask. "That warms my insides, it does. My pants are soaked."

"Man, are you that scared?" asked Jamie.

"No, of course not," answered the boy, indignant. "We waded across that cold creek." He passed his flask. "Here, Jamie, have a sup of 'Oh, Be Joyful.' Steadies the nerves and makes you fearless."

"I could sure use some of that fearlessness now. Pass it over, Ned." Jamie had already learned the names of many of the men around him. "Thank you kindly, dude."

"You sure do talk queerly," said Ned.

"Yeah, so I've been told." He knew he was too young to drink, but under the circumstances, what the heck? Jamie took a big mouthful, but could barely swallow it. It was home-brewed liquor and it tasted awful. "Well, I'm glad a few of the units used their brains and avoided the bridge."

"Wasn't exactly a cake walk, neither," said Ned. "Reb sharpshooters took a few potshots at us. Saw one of the men in my unit sink right under the water, and never come up again, neither."

Jamie shuddered and took another sip. Ned seemed to be about Rob's age. Where was Rob, Jamie wondered, feeling sudden, surprising tears spring to his eyes at the thought. What he wouldn't do to see that solemn little face again . . .

Jamie blinked his eyes and shook his head as if to clear it. There was no wind, yet he thought he saw the stalks of corn moving towards him.

"'Scuse me, Ned," said Jamie. "But either I've had too much of this 'Oh, Be Joyful' stuff, or those cornstalks are walking this way."

Ned laughed. "Just nerves. You have never seen the elephant, have you, Jamie?"

Jamie was sick and tired of this elephant talk. "Have you?"

Ned turned pale. "Lord, none of us in the 16th have ever been in a battle! Why, most of us loaded our muskets for the first time last night," he said, pointing his musket perilously close to Jamie's chest.

Jamie pushed Ned's musket away from him.

"Man, don't point that thing at me!" Jamie laughed nervously. "I should fit in just fine with you guys."

Underneath his cheerful facade, Jamie felt scared to the point of feeling sick. He reached for Ned's flask and took another long gulp of whiskey.

"Hey, I'm feeling more fearless by the minute, Neddie Boy."

Their conversation was interrupted by an officer on horseback ordering a complicated maneuver. Groaning, Jamie and Ned lurched to their feet. "Man, I wouldn't be able to do this even if I were sober."

The complex procedure was too much for the green recruits and they began bumping into each other, stumbling and cursing in the smoky corn field. Ned and Jamie, totally confused, stood still and waited for the maneuver to end.

"I wouldn't be able to do this on a parade ground," grumbled Ned. "And now he expects us to do this in a hilly corn field?"

If I'm going to have to do this ridiculous dance routine, at least let me do it to some decent music, thought Jamie. He surreptitiously slipped on his headphones.

But once again he thought he saw the cornstalks moving toward him. He grabbed Ned's arm. "The corn's moving, I tell you!" Just as he said this, a blood-curdling Rebel yell rang out and a hail of bullets whistled past his head. Jamie threw himself to the ground, then turned to say something to Ned, who was now nothing but a limp corpse with half a face. Jamie looked to the other side to find about half the men around him had been hit. Soldiers he had been standing around joking with only minutes before now lay on the ground, either crying out in agony or quiet forever.

The regiment nearest them, 4th Rhode Island, came up on their right.

"Help!" cried Jamie. "Over here, boys!"

But much to his horror, they began firing straight at him. In the high stalks of corn, it was difficult to tell friend from foe.

"Hey! I'm Union, dude! Don't shoot!"

"Hold your fire, men!" came the terse command. Two Union officers, one on each side of their flag bearer, moved cautiously forward to investigate, less than twenty feet from the Confederate line.

"You're Union?" one said. "Oh, yes, they're wearing blue!"

"Not them!" screamed Jamie. "They're—"

The Confederates blasted away, and the Union flag bearer fell to the ground, lifeless. One of the Union officers attempted to retrieve the fallen flag, but his hands were shaking so badly he dropped it. What was left of the 16th Connecticut turned on their heels and ran for their lives, the Rhode Islanders right behind them.

Jamie, without thinking, ran further out into the corn field to help the Union officer scoop up his country's flag.

****

Hill's Rebel warriors shot volley after volley through the cornstalks, continuing to shoot even as many of the Union soldiers fled.

Rob pulled out a round from his cartridge box, savagely biting the paper off with his teeth, then poured the powder down the muzzle. He pushed down the bullet with his thumb. He drew back the iron ramrod and pushed the projectile down. He pulled back the hammer, placing the percussion cap beneath it. He peered through the sights on his rifle, focusing on several Yanks who had not fled. Dodging bullets, they were trying to hold up the United States flag.

Rob started to squeeze the trigger, then froze. One of the men was a boy, and he had red hair that glinted in the sunlight.

"Jamie?"

He watched in horror as his kid brother fell.

****

Chapter 18

Clara Lights the Way

"Water! Water!"

Outside the barn, in the field, the bloody fingers of wounded men pulled at the women's skirts.

Sarah walked behind Clara Barton, helping to carry metal cups and pails of well water to the thirsty wounded. Many of the soldiers lay bleeding to death, their wounds dressed only with green leaves of corn, and this was their last word uttered on earth: "Water!"

Clara cradled a man's head in one hand as she lifted a cup of cool water to his parched lips. Sarah heard a whiz, then watched in horror as the man did a final death shudder. A stray bullet from the ongoing battle had torn right through Clara's sleeve—the one cradling the man's head—and struck him square in the chest.

"Are you all right, Miss Barton?" cried Sarah, rushing to Clara's side.

Miss Barton looked down at the sleeve of her dress. "I never did like this dress," she said, moving calmly to the next man.

As they continued moving down the line of men, giving them water, the chief doctor called to them.

"Miss Barton! Miss Singleton! I hate to leave you ladies alone with all these wounded men, but I've been called back to my regiment."

"It's all right, Dr. Dunn," Clara said stoically. "With Sarah's help and Cornie's, I will manage just fine."

"A few men in the Ambulance Corps are still here. And of course, you've still got ol' Sawbones."

Sarah looked at the doctor questioningly.

"The assistant surgeon. He's good. He can amputate twenty limbs in forty minutes without hardly wiping his saw."

Sarah forced a smile. "How . . . impressive."

The women watched as Dr. Dunn rode off in a whirl of dust.

"Well, Sarah, it's just you and me and Cornie."

A young soldier crawled over to them, his face covered with pus and blood. He pulled on the hem of Sarah's skirt. "Please, Miss, can you dig out the bullet in my cheek? I'm in dreadful pain. I just know I can bear it if you're the one who does it. You're beautiful like an angel."

Sarah stood frozen, but before she could make a decision Clara took over. She calmly wiped the blade of a pocket knife on her now bloodied apron. "I can dig it out as well as this young lady. Just close your eyes."

Sarah almost fainted with relief.

"Sarah, the men are starving and we're clean out of bread. Why don't you go over to the farmhouse and poke around in the cellar? See if you can find the men any vittles."

****

Sarah did not mind that the cellar was dark and damp. For a few minutes at least, she felt safe from the bombardment going on outside.

She discovered three boxes labeled "cornmeal." She pounced on them, tearing them open without a thought to her once pretty nails. Inside she found sifted yellow cornmeal. She dragged the boxes out a side door, one at a time. She was stronger than she had thought!

Sarah moved the boxes into the kitchen in the rear of the farmhouse and started up a fire. She found a large iron kettle, poured the cornmeal in, and hoisted it up over the fire. Soon, the fragrant smell of cornmeal gruel drifted through the farmhouse and out into the fields beyond.

Clara came in, face covered with soot, hair sticking out from her head, the hem of her skirt tucked up at her waist. "Well, grab some bowls and start ladling it out, dear. There's a line of wounded men clear back to the barn. Unless you want to take over assisting ol' Sawbones."

"No, that's all right, Miss Barton. That can be your job." She looked at how exhausted and shaky Clara was. "On second thought, let's switch."

As Clara ladled out bowls of cornmeal gruel to the starving men, Sarah steeled herself to return to the barn.

"Over here, girl!" yelled the surgeon. "We're out of chloroform and the men keep squirming around while I'm trying to saw."

Sarah stopped to wash her hands with lye soap and a bucket of water.

"What the devil are you doing, girl? This is no time to pretty yourself up! Just get over here!"

Sarah wiped her hands on her apron. She walked over and watched the surgeon try to hold a soldier steady with one dirty hand as he probed the man's bloody leg with his other filthy hand.

"I was not prettying myself up. It's a matter of basic hygiene. And it's something you might try yourself if you don't want to infect the man's wound with germs."

"Hmm? Germans? What are you talking about?" The big man glowered at Sarah. "Have you been to eight months of medical school, dearie? Well, I have, so I advise you to keep your ignorant girl opinions to yourself. Now I can't get the bullet out of this man's leg, so I'll have to cut the whole leg off. Hold him down, girl."

Sarah took a deep breath, then cradled the man's head in her arms. He started to scream and fight. She gave him a large swallow of the wine Miss Barton had brought. But Sarah—and the soldier—could still hear the saw cutting through flesh.

"Hush, little baby, don't say a word, Mama's goin' to buy you a mocking bird," sang Sarah in her sweetest voice. "And if that mocking bird don't sing . . . "

The man stopped his struggling and seemed to be listening to the sweet tune.

And so it went, Sarah singing and holding the men by the power of her voice, as the pile of arms and legs under the bench grew higher and higher.

At one point, the explosions from cannon fire came so close that the very walls of the barn shook. Everyone who could move ran for cover, including the surgeon. But Sarah continued cradling her patient, staunching the man's blood with cotton ripped from her petticoat, soothing him with her voice.

At the end of the bombardment, the surgeon crawled out from under a stack of hay. "Just looking for something I dropped," he stammered, pretending to peer into the haystack.

Sarah shot him a dirty look. "Not a needle, I hope," she muttered, as the orderlies hoisted up the next patient onto the bench.

****

The sound of fighting grew faint. As darkness gathered, Sarah heard only the moans and cries of the dying, punctuated by the relentless grind of the surgeon's saw.

"Confound it! I can't see what I'm cutting." The surgeon struggled to see by the flickering light of the last candle.

"That's our last one," said Sarah.

They stared at each other in horror.

Suddenly, Clara Barton burst through the door, holding a lantern, followed by her trusty Cornelius bearing armloads more of them.

"Getting too dark? I have more lanterns in my wagon."

The surgeon was so grateful he almost burst into tears. "You are an angel, Miss Barton . . . the angel of the battlefield."

"Oh, humbug," muttered Clara, busily lighting the lanterns and placing them around the barn.

"Come with me a minute, Sarah," she said, and the two of them went outside. "You must be exhausted, dear. Why don't you take a little rest? So many of the men have died, and the ones that haven't are being evacuated to decent field hospitals. Why, now that the fighting's over, I expect those ladies of the Sanitary Commission will descend upon us." Under her breath, she added, "Hmph—God help us, bunch of Ladies' Aid Society types."

"Well, actually, if you really don't need me, I would like to look for somebody . . . ," said Sarah.

"Oh, Sarah, had you a loved one fighting at the front?" asked Clara, all sympathy.

"Ummm . . . two, actually. Brothers."

"Oh, Lord help you, Sarah, you have two brothers in uniform! You must look for them at once, my dear. They might be needing your help. Begin your search now—it's safer to travel at night when the shooting's stopped."

"But how can I travel?"

As they were talking, one of the ambulance drivers whipped his horse, ready to depart.

"Where are you going?" called Clara, in her usual direct way.

"Down Hagerstown Turnpike, Ma'am," said the driver. "Going to pick up some more wounded to take to the nearest field hospital."

"Take this girl with you," ordered Clara. "She is clearly not a soldier and she may help you get through as you near Confederate lines."

She handed Sarah a loaf of bread and a small flask of wine, tucking them into the waistband of Sarah's deep apron. "Here, now. You share these with your brothers . . . the Lord will help you find them. And take one of my lanterns to light your way."

Then they looked at each other. They did not exchange another word, but simply squeezed each other's hands. Sarah looked down at her own hands, strong and capable ones . . . just like Clara Barton's.

****

Chapter 19

Among the Dead and Wounded

WEDNESDAY NIGHT, SEPTEMBER 17, 1862

Rob moved slowly through the shattered corn rows, his way lighted by a borrowed lantern.

It should have been easy to walk through the fields, as the once high stalks had been shaved down to a nub by artillery and gunfire. The problem now was to avoid stepping on the many bodies which littered the battlefield.

Through the darkness, Rob could hear the moans of wounded soldiers, many of them crying for water or to be shot and put out of their misery.

"Jamie? James Henry?"

Rob called out his brother's name again and again in the darkness.

Let him be alive, God, Rob prayed. I'll never be mean to him again. I swear it. He can have Sarah as his girlfriend. We can find Alexander Gardner and go back home. Just let him be alive.

A Rebel soldier bumped into him. "Excuse me," said Rob. "Have you seen a tall young Yank only fourteen years old? He's red haired, freckled, and he talks . . . um . . . kind of funny?"

"You're lookin' for a Yank?" asked the soldier.

Rob brushed away the tears running down his cheeks. "He's my brother."

The Reb soldier patted him on the back. "It don't seem to matter which side they're on anymore, does it? You're either dead or you're alive, and that's all that matters now."

"Well, I think he's alive. At least, I'm praying that."

". . . Thy kingdom come, Thy will be done . . . "

The words of the Lord's prayer drifted through the damp night air.

"Yep, there's a lot of prayin' goin' on tonight," said the Reb. "And while you're praying, pray that ol' Mac doesn't start fightin' us in the morning again."

"He won't," said Rob. "You can count on that."

The Reb looked at him in surprise. "How can you be so sure of that, boy?"

"Let's just say I'm good at predicting the future."

As they talked, a faint flash of lantern light appeared in the distance, growing closer and closer until it almost blinded them. When Rob opened his eyes again, he saw a dapper young man dressed in civilian clothes, carrying a notepad. "Excuse me, gentlemen, the name is George Smalley, reporter for *The New York Tribune*. Might I interview you for the article I'm writing? I need a Confederate point of view."

"You'd risk getting shot by one of our pickets— jest for a quotation for yer newspaper? You Yanks of the 'Bohemian Brigade' are plum crazy!" Disgusted, the Rebel left them.

A thought occurred to Rob. "If you're a reporter, Mr. Smalley, do you know if there are any photographers around here?"

"Can't wait to have your picture taken on the battlefield to show the folks back home, eh?"

Rob shook his head impatiently. "No, that's not it at all. I have urgent business with Alexander Gardner. He works for Mathew Brady."

"Well, we don't use pictures at the *Tribune*. But if you give me a good quote, I'll tell you what I heard which might help you find him."

"You tell me what you heard, then I'll give you a quote."

"All right, Johnny Reb. I heard Mr. Brady sent photographers here to cover the battle. Only they may not be here yet. They wouldn't want to be out here while the fighting was still going on. They have such delicate equipment. And how can you take a picture of fighting when you have such long exposure times, eh?"

"Thanks for the tip," said Rob. "Now you can ask me your question."

"How's it feel, when you're fighting a bloody battle like this?"

Journalism hasn't changed a bit, Rob thought—it was just as sensationalist back in the 1800's. "Not nearly as glorious as I thought it would feel," Rob said. "I almost shot my own brother."

"Hey, now, there's a good angle. Tell me about him. Is he a Union soldier?"

"Well, yes, sort of. We never got along. You know, we fought over the dumb things brothers always fight over. But now I'd give everything I ever owned just to see his smart-alecky little face again."

"That's funny, I got a similar quote from a young Union soldier. Except he talked real queerly."

Rob perked up. "How so?"

Smalley looked down at his notepad. "Let's see," he read, " 'My older brother's a Confederate. He used to drive me . . . nuts? But now I'd give everything I ever owned just to see that pain-in-the-ass . . . um . . . dude . . . again.'"

"Where is that boy? Was he all right?"

"He seemed to have taken a hit, but he wasn't dying," said Smalley. "I saw him by a big oak tree, near the wood fence," he pointed vaguely in the distance, "somewhere over there, I think."

Rob shook him. "Where? Show me!"

The reporter led him in the general direction. "Over there. Now if you don't mind, I have a story to file. And frankly, I'm getting a little nervous being here behind Reb lines."

"Show me exactly which tree you left him at, and where the nearest field hospital is, or I'll kill you!" screamed Rob. The reporter squirmed out of Rob's grasp and ran off.

"Hey, dude, hasn't there been enough killing around here?" called a hoarse, familiar voice.

"Jamie! Oh, my God, where are you?"

"Rob? Is that you? I'm over here!"

"Keep talking." Rob stumbled toward the voice, but then stopped, confused. It was like trying to find a ghost in the dark.

"Over here, by this tree . . . ."

Rob could barely hear him. "Come on, Jamie, give me that obnoxious whistle you used to make that could be heard for miles!" There was a long pause. Rob stood still, straining to hear. Suddenly, a long, drawn-out whistle pierced the air. Rob followed the sound, lantern in hand, then stumbled across something hard.

"Watch where you're going!"

Rob pointed his lantern downward. There, at his feet, was a white-faced Jamie, lying near a small puddle of blood, his head leaning against a tree. "Got some water, Rob? That whistling really dried me up bad."

Rob tenderly lifted his brother's head and poured water down his parched mouth from his canteen.

"Where's all that blood coming from?" asked Rob, frantically searching him, though afraid at what he might find. If the blood came from his arms or legs, he had a fighting chance of survival. But if it were from a minie ball in his back or his gut, or anywhere on his torso . . . well, Rob had read enough about Civil War medicine to know he'd be a goner.

"I think it's from my left leg," said Jamie, and Rob almost wept in relief. He bent down to inspect Jamie's leg. It took him almost two minutes before he found the gaping hole in the flesh near Jamie's ankle.

"It is just my leg, isn't it?"

"That's right, Jamie. I think the bullet may have gone right through and it's not even there anymore. You just need a doctor to clean out the wound a little, that's all." Rob tried not to think about amputations, to blot out the picture he had in his mind of Jamie with a stub instead of a leg.

"Hey, will you look at this?"

Jamie pointed to his Sony Walkman player, now smashed by a bullet. "Man, I knew music was important to me, but this is ridiculous! The darn thing saved my life!"

"Well, you don't need it now. We've got to get you to a doctor. And the less junk we have to carry the better." Rob threw the Sony Walkman set onto the field and dragged Jamie to his feet.

Jamie groaned in pain. "Man, when I think how I made fun of General Hooker's foot wound!"

"Here, just lean on me." Rob broke off a branch from the tree. "See, here's a crutch for you to lean on on your right side."

They hobbled along the road together, Rob desperately trying to support his brother's weight as much as possible. Jamie would start to collapse, but Rob pulled him up again, singing songs and telling jokes, trying to give Jamie the strength to keep moving.

"Oh, Suzanna," sang Rob, "oh don't you cry for—Jamie!"

His brother had stumbled, falling headlong to the ground.

"Come on, buddy, get up!" implored Rob, pulling on Jamie's arms.

"But where are we going? Where are you going to find a doctor?"

Rob forced himself to sound more confident than he felt. "Hey, don't you remember your history? After a battle, there'd be field hospitals set up all over the place. At churches, farmhouses, barns—everywhere."

"Yeah, but do you also remember what kind of medical care they had back then? Man, I don't want to have to bite on a bullet while they saw off half my leg!"

"They used ether or chloroform for anesthetics. I remember reading that."

"Yeah, if they were lucky enough to have any around," said Jamie. "And you're still forgetting about the . . . ," Jamie shuddered. He could not bring himself to say the word.

Rob had once researched the death rates from the various kinds of Civil War amputations. Amputations at ankle joint—a whopping 74 percent fatality rate—and that was on the Union side, which had better medical care! Rob decided to keep that particular statistic to himself.

"I won't let them do that to you. We'll just have them stop all the bleeding and then we'll get you back home."

"We're still missing a couple of people for that, aren't we? That Alexander dude and . . . Sarah."

They were both silent as they remembered the reason for their most recent estrangement.

"Jamie . . . I like Sarah and all that, but . . . "

"Rob . . . Sarah's okay, but . . . "

They both stopped as they realized they seemed about to say the same thing.

"You first," said Rob.

"No, you. Healthy men first."

Rob cleared his throat. "Well, when I thought maybe you were lying there dead somewhere, I prayed to God to let you live. I asked Him to let us go back home." He cleared his throat again. "I told God you could have Sarah."

Jamie laughed, in spite of his pain.

"And since when does Sarah Singleton let God— or anybody else—decide things for her?"

Rob started laughing too, then the laughter turned into tears and they hugged each other tightly.

"Come on, Jamie. Just drag yourself a little further and I promise you you're going to be all right."

As they hobbled along, they were almost run down by a Rebel ambulance wagon. The cart halted by a corn field and the orderlies lifted wounded men, using blankets as stretchers to drop them onto the precarious two-wheeled vehicle.

"Please help us," Rob pleaded.

They gave Jamie a cold look, noting his Union uniform. "We help our own first, soldier," one said.

"Well, maybe he got it at Harper's Ferry, like I did," said Rob, pointing to his own blue jacket.

They ignored him, continuing to load their wagon, one adding: "Hey, he's not so bad off. He can still hobble, can't he?"

Rob propped Jamie against a tree, then began to run after the cart to continue his argument. But noticing how the wagon jostled the wounded men so badly they writhed and screamed in agony, Rob decided on a new tack.

"Well, just tell me where he can get medical help and I'll get him there. He's only a kid, for God's sake, and he's my brother!"

One of the men gave him a sympathetic look and pointed towards a steepled building in the smoky distance. "See that old church flying the yellow flag? That's the sign of a doctoring place."

Rob squinted towards the smoking city. "Is it my imagination, or is the town burning?"

"Only part of it," shrugged one of the Rebs. "I wouldn't be so picky if I were you. I'm telling you, in the churches and schoolhouses they're helping wounded men."

"Who's helping them? Real doctors?" asked Rob.

"Oh, they're real, all right," replied the old ambulance driver. "Real saws an' everything."

****

Chapter 20

Beware Ol' Sawbones

WEDNESDAY AT MIDNIGHT, SEPTEMBER 17, 1862:

The rain poured down on Sarah as she dragged her exhausted body down the road towards Sharpsburg. She had hitched a ride part of the way in the ambulance wagon. But when they had stopped at a farm being used as a field hospital she had gotten out and started walking. She just could not stand the thought of seeing—and hearing and smelling—more of the surgeon's work.

She did not worry about crossing Confederate lines. She was beyond caring. She lifted her face to the rain, hoping the water would wash away the blood she felt steeped in. She ached to lie down and sleep. When she saw the steeple in the distance, she walked towards it.

Sarah shivered as she entered the church. Candles illuminated the stained-glass windows depicting Christ on the cross, giving the place a ghostly glow. Instead of prayers, Sarah heard the cries and moans of the wounded. Instead of incense, she smelled the stench of ether gas and death. Instead of worshippers kneeling, she saw bloody soldiers stretched out on boards, lying in distorted, unnatural positions. Most of them were

125

Confederates rather than Yanks, but otherwise the scene was much the same as it had been at the barn. And through it all, she heard the terrible and now familiar sound of the surgeon's saw, cutting back and forth, back and forth, through human flesh and bone.

Sarah thought of running out of the church. But then she remembered Clara Barton. She must pull herself together and help. She washed her hands in a bucket of water placed near the stone baptismal font, splashing the cool water over her face as well. She walked woodenly toward the sound of the surgeon's saw, wondering as she did so whether she was truly doing good by assisting in such butchery.

She entered a room with an operating table, glancing down at the bloody pile of arms and legs, hands and feet stacked underneath. "I can help you. I have experience . . . ," began Sarah, but the gray-haired surgeon, his white coat stained with blood and vomit, barely gave her a glance. He just gave her a curt nod, his eyes glazed and vacant looking. Sarah wondered if he was feeling the effects of the ether. Great, she thought, a "doctor" with dirty hands and filthy clothes who's high on ether gas.

She watched the surgeon tie off a soldier's arteries with silk thread, just above a stump where a leg had been only minutes before.

Sarah began feeling light-headed herself, whether from the horrifying sights, the ether, or lack of sleep she did not know. In a fog, she saw the now legless soldier carried away and another put down on the table in his place. Vaguely, she perceived the soldier thrashing around, struggling to get away. She began her old routine of cradling the head gently in her arms. Then she dropped it on the operating table with a thud.

"James Henry!"

****

Jamie looked up at her with a weak grin. "Are you always this gentle with your patients?"

Sarah began coughing violently.

The surgeon glared at her. "Well, go and get your-self a drink of water, girl. If you're coughing like that, you won't do me much good. I'll go outside and get one of those orderlies to help me hold him down."

He gave Jamie a stern look as Sarah continued to cough. "Now you stay right here." He turned to go, then changed his mind. "I think I'll make sure of that." He tied Jamie to the table with a a large canvas belt before he left.

"Quick, get me out of here!" said Jamie, the mo-ment the surgeon left.

Sarah undid the belt and helped Jamie up, as Rob burst into the room. "Oh, my God! Sarah Singleton! Am I glad to see you!"

"Help me get your brother out of here," she said, wasting no time in greeting him. With Sarah holding him on one side and Rob on the other, Jamie limped out of the operating room.

"I don't know, guys," said Rob, looking at all the blood coming from Jamie's leg. "Maybe we should let the doctor have a go at Jamie, after all."

"No," said Sarah. "I've seen what these butchers do. With their filthy hands, they try to fish the bullet out of you. And when that doesn't work, or if they can't find the minie ball, they just chop off your limbs with their filthy, blood-covered saw. And this Confederate Sawbones," she added, jerking her thumb towards the surgeon who had just left, "is drunk on ether, besides!"

Jamie shuddered at his close call, as Sarah tore off his pant leg and washed off his lower leg with the water at the baptismal font.

"There . . . that will clean it out a bit."

Rob and Jamie looked at her, impressed.

"I've had a lot of practice. Now let's split this joint!"

Jamie winced, tenderly touching his ankle. "I wish you hadn't said that." He looked around nervously. "Do you think Ol' Sawbones will come after me?"

Sarah laughed bitterly. "Are you kidding? He has so many wounded to chop up, he's hardly going to notice one more or one less. Besides, he's high as a kite!"

With the painfully limping Jamie in the center, they hobbled out of the church and into the graveyard in the back.

Jamie shuddered in the rainy midnight chill, staring at the wet white graves shimmering in the moonlight. "Whoa, no more *Goosebumps* books for me!"

Rob smiled at his brother. "I'm glad you still have your sense of humor."

Sarah pointed to a mausoleum which would protect them from the rain. They got Jamie over to it. Sarah patted the cold stone steps of the tomb. "Sit down," she said, pulling out her flask of wine. Before Jamie knew what she was doing, she poured some of the wine directly over his wound.

"Owww! You're burning me!"

"Good," said Sarah. "The wine went right through the hole. That's almost as good as a modern antiseptic."

Sarah ripped off a piece of her now shredded petticoat and wound it tightly around Jamie's wound.

"There. That will stop the bleeding for awhile. You're lucky the bullet went straight through you."

They drank the rest of the wine. It warmed their insides and eased Jamie's pain. Then Sarah tore off some bread.

As Jamie leaned up against her, she noticed with relief that Rob no longer seemed to be jealous.

"Now what we have to do is find Alexander Gardner," said Sarah, "and find him fast, before infection sets in. We've got to get Jamie back to modern times." She turned to Rob. "Unless you're still set on living in this bloody nightmare."

"No," said Rob. "I've had enough. You're right, Sarah. In a modern hospital, Jamie'd be fine. They'd just pump him full of antibiotics."

Jamie smiled weakly. "Always trust Sarah for a plan. But one little problem, dudes . . . "

"How do we find Alexander Gardner?"

****

Chapter 21

Where Oh Where Is the What's-It Wagon?

THURSDAY MORNING, SEPTEMBER 18, 1862:

Waiting for the dawn to light their way, the three talked.

"I was told Mathew Brady sent photographers to cover the battle," said Rob. "Do you think Alexander's here?"

"Last time I saw him was back in Frederick," said Sarah.

"Why didn't you stay with him?" asked Jamie, curious more than angry.

"It's a long story," said Sarah, looking down at her hands. "Let's just say I met Clara Barton . . . and I'll never be the same again. How do you feel, Jamie?"

"Not quite as weak," Jamie said. "I think your petticoat has stopped the bleeding for now."

"Then we'd better get moving," said Sarah. "We've got to find Alexander before your wound gets infected."

"But where are we going?" asked Jamie, his face grimacing in pain as he moved.

"Well," said Sarah, "I'm just guessing but maybe he'll go back to the same places he photographed before. Now think, guys," said Sarah, "like the Civil War experts I know you are. What were the most famous Brady—I mean, Alexander Gardner—photographs of Antietam?"

"Well, I remember the famous one of Dunker Church," said Rob. "A bunch of dead artillerists, lying in front of their cannon, with that shell-pocked white church in the background."

"Dunker Church, that's a long walk from here, isn't it?" asked Sarah. "Any other ones?"

"How about that picture of the dead horse?" suggested Rob. "That horse almost looked like he was asleep."

"Where was it taken?" asked Sarah.

"I don't know," said Rob. "You can just see some woods in the background."

"Great," said Sarah. "Could be West Woods, East Woods, North Woods, or any other woods near the battleground."

"Weren't there photos of Burnside Bridge?" asked Jamie. "But wait, those could have been shot days after the battle. Because there weren't any bodies in the pictures! Geez," Jamie added, bitterness in his voice, "now that I've seen that guy in action, I can't believe they named that bridge after him."

"A. P. Hill. . . ," said Rob, shuddering as he remembered. "Now there was a sweetheart."

"Hey, at least he was effective. Let me tell you about Little Mac . . . ," started Jamie.

"Guys, focus! You can reminisce later, when we're back home, okay?"

"Focus . . . focus . . . That reminds me of a picture," said Rob. "Taken by Alexander Gardner—now that I know it was him. It was hanging right in his sutler's tent, remember? In the foreground—in focus—

are all those Reb bodies piled up in Sunken Road, later known as Bloody Lane. In the background, slightly blurred as if they had moved, you can see a couple of Union soldiers."

"So you think that was taken soon after the battle?" asked Sarah, excited.

"Well, not more than two days later, 'cause the bodies were still . . . intact. Not decomposed or anything."

"And not buried yet," said Jamie, watching as a straggling, demoralized-looking unit of Rebel soldiers carrying picks and shovels approached, followed by a cart loaded with corpses. "Phew," he said, holding his nose. "They better start burying those guys fast."

"Don't you see?" said Sarah, really excited now. "Alexander must be rushing to the battlefield as fast as possible. Because as soon as they bury these guys, there'll be nothing dramatic to photograph!"

"Good point. Hey, dudes," called out Jamie to the burial detail. "Where's Bloody Lane?"

They looked at him as if he were crazy.

" 'The Sunken Road,' " added Rob. "You know, where D. H. Hill's men hunkered down about mid-day of the battle."

"Oh, so that's what you mean! Bloody Lane, eh? That's a good name for it." One of the men laughed bitterly. "You're going sightseeing over in Yank territory?"

"We're looking for someone," said Sarah.

"It'll likely be a dead someone, if you're looking over there. I hear our men's bodies are piled up six deep in that hole."

"But where is it?" asked Sarah, impatient.

"Down Boonsboro Turnpike a couple miles, till you hit a fork in the road. Can't miss it, Ma'am . . ." Again, the bitter laugh. "Jest follow your nose." The man covered his face with a handkerchief, as he motioned to his men to move the cart filled with corpses.

"Come on, guys, let's go," said Sarah, helping Jamie to his feet.

One of the Rebels stopped to talk to Jamie. "Listen, Yank, maybe I should warn you 'bout something, especially you bein' with a lady an' all . . . . "

"Watch out for our sharpshooters!"

****

They approached Federal lines.

"What on earth are you doing?" asked Sarah, surprised to see Jamie squirming out of his blue jacket and throwing it on the ground.

"If there are Reb snipers, the last thing I need is another minie ball. Now help me out of these pants. Cut them off, if you need to."

"Don't worry about the trousers," said Rob, squirming out of his blue jacket acquired at Harper's Ferry. "They're so bloody, they're not blue anymore."

Soon they passed another burial detail, this one a Federal unit.

"Excuse me," called Rob. "Have you men seen any photographers?"

"What?" said one of the men, confused. "Pho . . . what?"

"What we mean is," said Sarah, "have you guys seen an oddly-shaped, black-hooded buggy, drawn by a horse? Driven by a big burly man with a dark beard, dark eyes, and long hair? Who speaks as if he's from Scotland?"

"Oooh, I think I know what you mean," said a pick-carrying soldier. "One of those 'What's-it wagons' that take pictures?"

"Uhhh . . . that's right," said Rob. "Well . . . have you seen the 'What's-it wagon?'"

"I think I did see him drive by late yesterday afternoon."

"Where were you?" asked Sarah.

"Why, over by McClellan's headquarters, now that I think about it," drawled the man with maddening slowness. "But he talked about heading over in this direction to take some pictures, as I recall." He looked at the filthy teenagers in their bloody clothes and scratched his head. "You young people want your pictures taken now?"

****

Chapter 22

Bloody Lane

THURSDAY AFTERNOON, SEPTEMBER 18, 1862:

As Rob, Jamie and Sarah approached "Sunken Road," they began to understand where the name came from—it was a long sunken ditch ground into the dirt from years of wagon travel. Only now it contained piles of corpses, their bodies contorted from violent death.

Suddenly, the sound of musket fire rang out.

"Oh, no! I thought the battle was over!" Jamie exclaimed, as they ducked into a nearby grove of trees.

The three watched as Union pickets dove for cover right into the Bloody Lane. "Man!" whistled Jamie. "Those Feds dove right on top of all those dead Rebel dudes."

A white flag emerged over the Bloody Lane.

The shooting stopped as suddenly as it had begun, as an answering white flag waved from the Rebel side.

Soon, the land around the sunken road was filled with Union and Rebel soldiers, mixing freely, exchanging rations, bartering with one other. The brogue of the Irish Brigade mixed freely with the twang of the Mississippi, as the men who'd been trying to kill each

135

other began joking and chatting, getting friendlier by the minute.

"You see how crazy this war is?" asked Jamie. "These guys would be best friends if they roomed together in a dorm."

"Or maybe they'd be brothers," said Rob, "like us."

But the gay social hour was interrupted by the sound of horses' hooves, as a troop of Federal cavalry suddenly appeared on a nearby rise.

The three watched as the Rebs ran towards them in desperate fear. "Don't shoot!" cried one, over his shoulder, as he ran for his life.

"Run, Johnny, run," called a gentle Irish voice. "Do not fear. For we'll not harm ye, my friend."

And not a single bullet was fired.

****

Among the trees in the orchard, Rob, Jamie, and Sarah stayed hidden. The stench coming from the lane was horrid. Clouds of insects buzzed near the bodies and crows circled around and around in the clear blue sky. Sarah pulled a forgotten flacon of perfume from her pocket.

"What are you doing?" asked Rob.

Sarah emptied the last few drops onto her wrist, then tossed the tiny bottle to the ground. She pressed her nose to her wrist. "Phew," she said, inhaling deeply.

Many of the trees had been splintered by explosions and gunfire. But some of them still bore fruit. Rob climbed one of them and dropped apples down to supplement their now meager bread supply.

Periodically, the Rebels would start shooting from inside a nearby barn. In a desultory style, as if they were really too tired to care, the Union pickets would fire back. Then all would be silence again, except for the moans of dying men.

The three took turns watching the Bloody Lane, just in case Gardner's wagon should suddenly appear.

As darkness fell, they heard the distant sounds of an army moving—marching feet and rumbling artillery wagons.

"What's that?" asked Sarah, nervous.

"That's the Rebels retreating," said Rob.

"The battle's been over for twenty-four hours. Why didn't they leave earlier?" asked Sarah.

"That's Robert E. Lee's way of saving face," Rob explained. "If his army had fled right after the battle, it would look as if McClellan had a big victory."

"Yeah, but it won't help," said Jamie. "Knowing 'Big Mac,' he'll brag about his big victory, anyhow. Just wait till Lincoln cans him, though!"

" 'Big Mac,' not 'Little Mac'?" asked Rob, laughing.

"Yeah, that's what I used to call him. Figured it'd make him sound big. Not that he needed any help in that particular department," Jamie added. "Though that reminds me, a 'Big Mac' sure would taste good right now."

"Have a piece of bread," said Sarah. "How's your foot?"

"Really starting to hurt," said Jamie, wincing.

"It's probably getting infected," said Sarah. "Alexander had better get here soon."

Towards morning, they were startled awake by the sound of artillery.

"What now?" cried Sarah, alarmed.

"Oh, that's just Jamie's pal 'Big Mac'," said Rob. "He had a battery put up on the hill, just to fire cannon at the retreating Rebs. Sort of to thumb his nose at them. It's not like he could really hit them now. The Rebs all left during the night."

"It's a good thing we got out of town when we did," said Sarah.

Eventually the firing stopped. The three closed their ears, shut their eyes and one by one fell asleep.

Sarah woke to the sound of a horse-drawn carriage and a most familiar voice.

"Well, come now, Mr. Gibson! We dunna have all day. We must be takin' our pictures while the light is good!"

****

Chapter 23

Just One Happy Family

FRIDAY, SEPTEMBER 19, 1862

There, by the Bloody Lane, stood the horse-drawn photographic wagon tethered to a nearby tree, a large camera mounted on a tripod, and a square black tent only about four feet by four feet. A man's long legs stuck out from under the cloth of the camera.

"Alexander?" asked Sarah, impatiently pulling back the cloth.

A young man blinked back at her in surprise.

"No. J. B. Gibson. Who are you, might I ask?"

"Sarah Singleton." She looked around wildly. "Isn't Alexander Gardner here?"

Stooping, a bulky-looking man emerged from the little black tent.

"Alexander!" cried Sarah, hugging him. "You're here!"

"Well, o' course I am, lass, I got to do the pictures right this time! An' how is Clara Barton?"

"She's wonderful."

139

Gardner gave her a warm smile. "An' so were you, I have no doubt about that, bonnie lass. Did you find your friends?"

Holding on to each other tightly for support, Rob and Jamie came limping out of the apple orchard.

"Ah, there they are! I see Jamie's got a bit of a problem with his leg. Were you hit with a minie ball, young friend?"

"Yeah, and it's starting to hurt a lot," said Jamie.

They all looked down at the wound which was starting to turn an ugly black color.

"You need modern antibiotics, and you need them fast," said Sarah. "Alexander, you must get us back!"

He turned his sharp eyes on Rob. "An' you all agree to it now?"

"Yes," said Rob. "It was a horrible war, brother against brother." He put an arm protectively around his brother.

"Yeah, the past stinks," said Jamie, wrinkling up his nose at the stench coming from the corpses in Bloody Lane.

"Aye, but it will make a powerful picture, won't it now?" said Alexander, eying the bodies, over a hundred of them, neatly stacked up in rows just as they fell.

"How would you like us to pose?" asked Sarah. "Same position as before?"

"Hold your horses, Sarah girl, 'tis not quite that simple."

"What's the catch?" asked Rob, terrified that they couldn't go back. If anything happened to his brother . . .

"When you time traveled here in the first place, were you not all wearin' something original from this historic period?"

They all nodded.

"Well, to reverse time travel, you need something from your modern times, don't you see?"

"Darn it, Rob!" cried Jamie. "Why did you throw out my Sony Walkman?"

"Have you nothing on your person from your own time?"

"Wait a minute," said Jamie, a sly look coming over his face. "My underwear! Dirty as can be—and just as modern!"

"I'm sorry, guys," said Rob. "Mr. Hard-core here has nothing modern on him!"

He blinked away a tear. "Ouch!" Rob cupped his hand over his eye.

"What's wrong?" asked Sarah.

"Oh, just my contact lens. Something blew in it, that's all."

His mouth dropped open as he realized what he had just said. "My contact lenses! They're definitely a modern invention!"

Sarah smiled sadly. "You guys will just have to go back without me!"

To comfort her, Rob drew her close. "No, Sarah, we wouldn't do that. Besides, we can't, can we, Mr. Gardner?"

Alexander nodded his head. "That's right, lad. You have to travel as a threesome, just as you came."

Rob sniffed near Sarah. "Even with all these corpses, something smells sweet," he noted. "Almost like flowers."

"Oh, that," said Sarah, smelling her wrist. "It's just my perfume. I put on my last few drops to hide the stink from Bloody Lane."

"Wait a minute! That perfume! I'll bet it's as modern as my contact lenses!" exclaimed Rob. "Wouldn't that count, Mr. Gardner?"

Alexander beamed, nodding his big head. "It should do just fine," he said. "All right, children, you three must pose."

"But wait," said Rob, "can't you come back with us?" He pointed to Gibson, who was carefully pulling equipment from the wagon. "Your assistant could take a picture of all four of us, couldn't he?"

Alexander shook his head. "No, lad, I have nothing modern to wear and not a thing from your time period to hold in me hands."

"But how did you get to the reenactment where we first met?" Alexander shrugged his shoulders. "I dunna know, lad. Perhaps in my way of thinking I was ahead of my time. But I've had enough of this time travelin,' anyhow. I belong in the past."

"But what about your sutler's tent at the reenactment? And all those wonderful pictures hanging on the wall?" asked Rob.

"I'll give you my photographs as a little present, lad. They're for you and your brother and that fine lass of yours too, to share among you." He gave them a wink. "Those pictures might be worth a great deal of money in your time, eh?"

"Now . . . what do you people say? Cheeese?"

****

"Think modern thoughts," said Jamie, as he held tightly to his brother's arm on one side and to Sarah's arm with the other.

"I will," said Rob. "No more fixating on the past for me!"

Sarah smiled. "Oh, I wouldn't go that far. You still have to pass your history exam this semester!"

Rob smiled. Then Jamie smiled, even though his foot throbbed.

"Just one happy family!" exclaimed Alexander. "Now hold for the count of fifteen."

****

Minutes later, Alexander held back the flap of the small darkroom tent.

"Do you think all three of you can squeeze in there together?"

"Sure we can!" exclaimed Sarah. She blew him a farewell kiss, as the three entered the tent.

"Just do everythin' the same as you did before," said Alexander.

"Everything?" asked Jamie guiltily, remembering the sneaky way in which he had tried to kiss Sarah.

"Everything?" asked Rob guiltily, remembering how hard he had punched his brother and how he had longed to kill him.

"Everything?" asked Sarah guiltily, remembering how childish and weak she had been to cry about ruining the picture and then fainting.

Alexander laughed. "All right, not everything. Just swoosh some of the developer solution in the air. I've already poured it over the glass plate negative."

"And throw the glass plate on the floor," added Sarah. "Just in case."

Inside the dark tent, Rob groped his way over to the tub of chemicals. Jamie helped him spill out the liquid. Sarah threw down the plate. Then the three held each other tightly in the pitch black tent. They had to, it was that cramped. But more than that, they wanted to. For the love the three of them shared for each other was as strong as the smell of the acid.

The tent began spinning around them.

"Wheee!" cried Sarah.

"Here we go, dudes!" said Jamie.

"I love you guys!" said Rob.

"I love you too, man!" said Jamie. "See ya back in . . ."

****

" . . . the sutler's tent?"

Rob finished Jamie's sentence, as he looked around just to make sure that that was indeed where they were.

"Yup, that's where we are!" said Jamie. He walked over to a photograph hanging on the wall. "Look! There's Bloody Lane!"

"Jamie!" shrieked Sarah. "You're walking!"

"Well, so I am." Jamie leaned over to examine his leg. "Whoaa, not even a scratch where the minie ball went in!"

"What's that?" asked Sarah, pointing to a dot.

"A freckle," said Jamie.

Rob came up next to Jamie to examine the photograph. He suddenly caught his breath, then pointed with a shaking finger at the lower right-hand corner.

"Photograph by Alexander Gardner," it said in small silver writing.

"Man, I don't remember seeing that before," said Jamie.

"That's because it wasn't there. Don't you see that's why Alexander Gardner had to go back to the past? To get the credit he deserved," said Rob.

"Whoa, that's too spooky, dudes. Get me out of here."

Suddenly, they heard the sound of a cannon. Rob cringed. "Oh, no!" he cried.

"Don't worry," said Sarah, patting his arm. "It's just the reenactment, remember? It must still be going on."

"I don't think I could stand reenacting battles of war after what we've been through," said Rob.

"Yeah, man," agreed Jamie. "I've seen the elephant! Now I just want to go home."

"Well, let's just watch it as spectators, then," insisted Sarah. "You know, for old times' sake."

Still in their historic period clothing, they sauntered over to the battlefield, joining all the camera-carrying tourists in shorts. They stood in the crowd, safely behind the spectators' rope.

"Hey, Jamie!" pointed out Rob, laughing. "Look at that guy over there with headphones on! He's as 'farb' as you used to be!"

Jamie joined in the laughter, watching the man move rhythmically as if listening to music.

Jamie's laughter died in his throat. For the man wore a derby hat and a red checkered shirt. And when he turned around, Jamie saw a fat cigar in his mouth.

"Ummm . . . Rob? Sarah? Did either of you guys happen to keep the negative?"

Sarah laughed. "I did. I thought it'd be a good souvenir." She reached into her pocket and pulled it out.

There the three of them were, smiling and holding each other.

And in the background, slightly blurred as if he had moved, was Allan Pinkerton, examining the Sony Walkman in his hands.

****